White Cloud Retreat

A Cedar Bay Cozy Mystery

BY

DIANNE HARMAN

Published by: Dianne Harman
www.dianneharman.com

Interior, cover design and website by
Vivek Rajan Vivek
www.vivekrajanvivek.com

ISBN: 978-1506130194

CONTENTS

ACKNOWLEDGMENTS

First of all, I want to thank all of my readers who have made this series so popular, I truly appreciate your taking the time and spending the money to read them. I always appreciate your thoughts about this book or any of my others. I'd love to hear from you. Here's my email address: dianne@dianneharman.com.

Secondly, I want to extend a special thanks to Vivek Rajan Vivek (www.vivekrajanvivek.com) for the fabulous book covers he creates, his unending sound advice, and his taking the time to answer the gazillion questions I always have. I not only think of him as my editor, formatter, and marketing guru, I think of him as a friend and highly recommend him.

Finally, I want to thank my husband, Tom, for his support, belief in me, and love. Without him, none of this would be possible. Thanks!!!

CHAPTER ONE

Kelly drove up the road leading to the White Cloud Retreat Center, looking forward to taking a yoga and meditation class from Zen Master Scott to try and get rid of some of the stress she was feeling.

The last few months are catching up with me what with the holidays and the two murders in the Cedar Bay area that I helped Sheriff Mike solve. I can just imagine how busy the next few weeks are going to be while I try to find the time to put the final touches on our wedding plans. It's only three weeks away. I am so ready for this class. This is my wedding gift to myself — weekly yoga classes.

She smiled thinking of the wedding present that her fiancé, Mike, had given her. He was the local county sheriff and after she'd helped him solve the recent Jeff Black murder case he'd given her a little female yellow Labrador retriever puppy. The young dog had already claimed a soft spot in her heart. Since Mike and her other dog, Rebel, were continuing to bond together, it was a good thing she had a new dog. The little puppy with the chocolate brown eyes was now four months old and Kelly had named her "Lady." She knew it was probably a trite name, but it just seemed appropriate for a female dog that carried herself with such dignity. She could almost feel her soft fur and warm, wet puppy kisses whenever she thought of Lady. It brought a wide smile to her face.

True to its name, puffy white clouds had settled on the upper portion of the Retreat Center and Kelly could see people working in the vineyard, pruning the dormant vines and getting them ready for the spring growth.

She parked her minivan and took her yoga mat out of the trunk. Scott only taught once a week and from the number of people walking up to the front door, it was pretty clear his class was very popular with the students. She entered the room where the class was going to be held and spread her mat on the floor, smiling and nodding to several people she knew. Kelly glanced at the clock and realized she had a little time to do some stretches and warm-up exercises before the class started.

When Scott walked into the class he smiled at her as well as at a number of other students. Kelly had taken classes over the years from Scott and they shared a mutual love of food. He occasionally stopped by the coffee shop she owned, Kelly's Koffee Shop, and when he did he usually brought her a bottle of White Cloud Pinot Noir wine from the Center's vineyard.

Scott was one of the most admired and sought-after Zen Masters in the United States. People came from all over the country to take seminars from him or be a part of the residential training programs he conducted several times a year. His brother Luke, who, according to Scott, had been a successful securities broker in New York, had recently quit his job because of burn-out and had come to the Center to help Scott run the rapidly growing non-profit business. Although the Center employed seven priests and five nuns who handled a lot of the Center's day-to-day work, Scott still couldn't keep up with the number of people who wanted to study with him. He rarely wore Zen Buddhist robes, preferring blue jeans and flannel shirts which barely covered his growing girth. His appearance was completely unconventional for what one thought a Zen Master should look like.

I can't believe he's so revered in the Zen and yoga circles throughout the country. He's got to be one of the most down-to-earth people I've ever met. I believe he's celibate, but as charismatic as he is, that must present some problems. She looked around the room and noticed that the first three rows of students seated on their yoga mats waiting for the class to begin were women. *I'm not surprised. He's a totally charming and totally unique man.*

Women adore him, but men like him just as much.

Scott rang a small hand-held brass bell, indicating that the class was starting. For the next hour he led the assembled students in a series of physical movements the yogis called asanas which worked every part of their bodies.

At the conclusion of the regular class, an Italian looking man two rows ahead of her raised his hand. Kelly didn't recall seeing him in any of the classes she'd taken before, although it had been awhile since she'd been to the Center. "Yes, Guido," Scott said.

"Are we going to have the walking meditation today? I remember last week you mentioned we might."

"You're a step ahead of me, Guido. I was just getting ready to announce a five minute bathroom break. Please meet back here and then we'll go outside for the walking meditation."

A few minutes later he told the assembled students to follow him. "It's a sunny day and as Guido said, I told you last week that if it was sunny today, I thought that rather than our usual sitting meditation, we'd end the class by doing a walking meditation in the forest behind the buildings. Some of you have done them before in the forest. It's really one of my favorite ways to meditate. If you're new to a walking meditation, simply put your hands together and mindfully be aware of each step you take.

"If you haven't been in our forest meditation area yet, you're in for a treat. Each path is unique and has its own name such as Serenity, Peace of Mind, Bodhi, Enlightenment, and Wisdom, to name a few. There are a large number of designated and named paths in the forest and I think we can each walk down a separate path and quietly meditate. Take a moment and choose the one that speaks to you. At the end of each path you'll find a bench which overlooks a small pond or beautiful green foliage of some type. Stop and sit on the bench for a few minutes while you complete your meditation. Take time to enjoy the peace and tranquility of the forest. You'll hear me strike the big gong in front of the center at the end of fifteen minutes. Please come back here when you hear the gong. Let's go."

The students followed him on a dirt path to the forest's edge and dispersed in silence, each one looking inward. Kelly walked to a path on the far right that led into the forest with its deep green ferns and dappled sunlight. Out of the corner of her eye, she saw Guido and a woman with bright red hair hurrying to get to the paths near her. It was a beautiful and peaceful setting. The path Kelly chose was marked with a sign that said "Tranquility." She put her hands together and began slowly walking.

Seems like an awful long time has gone by, Kelly thought. *I wonder how long it's been.*

When she'd arrived at the Center, she'd taken her cell phone and keys with her, leaving her purse locked in the van. As she prepared to go on the walking meditation she'd slipped both of them in the pocket of her yoga pants. Now she took her phone from her pocket and looked at the time. Twenty-five minutes had gone by and she hadn't heard the sound of the gong being struck.

Well, I must have missed it. I was pretty focused on the walking meditation and keeping my mind clear of outside distractions. Guess I overdid it. Better get back to the Center. Obviously I'm late. I think this path to the left is shorter and will take me back to the Center a little faster rather than trying to retrace my steps on the Tranquility path.

She hurried along the dimly lit forest path which was thickly littered with soft needles that had fallen from the cedar trees. She hadn't gone very far on the shortcut path when she saw a large shape on the ground to her left. *Oh my gosh,* she thought. *I've heard there are black bears in some of these forests. I hope that isn't one.* She remembered hearing somewhere that if you ever encountered a bear, you should stand perfectly still. Kelly didn't move a muscle while she looked at the shape. She suddenly realized it wasn't a bear at all, but instead what she was looking at was a human form. She walked over to it, and gasped. It was Zen Master Scott. Blood was pooling around his body and Kelly could clearly see a bullet hole in his head. He was dead.

CHAPTER TWO

Jim and Ellie Duncan were at home reading the Bible like they did every Saturday morning when the phone rang. Jim reached over and picked it up.

"Hello, this is Jim Duncan."

"Hi, Jim. This is Leroy down at the Cascades Electric dispatch center. Sorry to have to call you out on a Saturday, but your name was at the top of the rotation list for emergency call out duty. We've got two problems that Charlie over in maintenance and repair wants you to take care of today."

"Okay. Where does he want me to go?"

"The first one is out at the Bar Z cattle ranch and feed lot. They had a lightning strike last night on the transformer next to their feed lot and they've lost all their power. They've got 1,500 cattle in the feed lot that are all fed using an electrical powered conveyor system that brings the feed directly to each holding pen. To say they have a big problem that needs to be fixed as fast as possible is an understatement. Their ranch is about twenty-five miles north of Cedar Bay off of Henderson Road."

"Yeah, I know where it is. I've driven by it a number of times. It's the one where you can smell the feed lot three miles before you get there and can see it. What's the other job?"

"We have an ongoing problem out at the White Cloud Retreat Center. Their lights keep flickering on and off because of some kind of power interruption. The maintenance records indicate you were out there last week and did some repair work in their utility vault, but apparently that didn't do the trick, because they're still having problems. Charlie wants you to check out the power lines located in the right of way that leads from our substation to the Center. The substation is located about a mile from the Center and the right-of-way cuts directly over the ridge behind the substation and then goes through the forest to where it terminates at the Center. Charlie thinks maybe some tree branches are coming in contact with our power lines and causing the intermittent electrical outages at the Center.

"He wants you to take one of our big four wheel drive service trucks that are equipped with both a power wench and a cherry picker basket. The ground in the right-of-way where the lines are located is relatively smooth and you shouldn't have any trouble driving the truck in the right-of-way while you look for overhanging tree limbs that need to be trimmed back. You can use the cherry picker basket to get up high enough to trim any tree limbs that might need to be trimmed."

"Sure. I can do that."

"Charlie said for me to tell you he's sorry about this, but he's shorthanded today and doesn't have any other maintenance crew members available that can go with you on these two jobs. He wants you to do the Bar Z ranch job first as it's the most important of the two. He said you should probably be finished with that job by 2:00 and then you should be on site and ready to work on the Center job by 3:00."

"Sounds like a good plan to me, Leroy. By the way, I worked on some tree removals in that right-of-way that leads to the Center about three years ago. When I was there, I saw a female black bear with two cubs and she wasn't very happy about my presence in the area. That whole area is prime black bear habitat and because I'm going to be working alone, think I'll take my gun with me for protection. I know my little ol' .22 pistol can't kill a bear, but it sure might put a scare into one and give me time to get away."

"Better think twice before you take your gun with you. You know company policy prohibits employees from having a loaded firearm in their possession at any time while they're on duty, and that includes while you're working alone in a company truck.

"Okay, I get it. Tell Charlie I'll do my best to find the cause of the service interruption at the Center and fix it, however, between you and me, I really don't care if they never get their electrical service properly restored. Those people that run the Center, especially the guy that calls himself the Zen Master, Scott Monroe is his name, are evil non-believers who are doing everything they can to destroy the work of our Lord. The next time God delivers a lightning bolt like the one that hit the transformer over at the Bar Z, I hope it hits Zen Master Scott right on top of his head. If God doesn't take care of him pretty soon, then some earthly human needs to take him out and eliminate this cancer that's growing in our community."

"Whoa, Jim, be careful what you say. This is your old buddy Leroy talking and let me tell you if Charlie ever heard you say something like that he'd have you back digging utility trenches by hand or worse yet, it could get you fired. Don't forget the company motto we have here at Cascades Electric Company, 'The customer has the power; we provide the service.' See you later Jim. The big service truck is loaded and waiting for you in the maintenance yard."

I'm going to take my gun with me. I don't care what the company policy says and anyway, I might need it for my personal protection. And yes, if I saw that evil Zen Master out in the forest, I wouldn't mind taking a pot shot at him just to scare him or better yet maybe I ought to blow his head off. Good riddance to that fountain of evil in our community. It would be for the best and I'm sure the Lord would understand and forgive my actions.

"Ellie," Jim said as he stood up, "I've got to work today. I'll be back in time for dinner.

CHAPTER THREE

Kelly grabbed her phone from her pocket and with a trembling hand, punched in Mike's number. He picked up the call immediately. "How was class, Sweetheart?" he asked.

"You need to come to the Retreat Center right now," she said shakily. "Scott's been murdered. I just discovered his body in the forest behind the Center. Hurry!"

"I'm on my way. Don't hang up. Okay, I'm in my patrol car and heading out. I'll be there in a few minutes. Tell me specifically where you are."

She was dazed with an uncomprehending look on her face as she stood staring at Scott's body, the phone in her hand. "Kelly, answer me," she heard Mike saying. "Tell me where you are. Are you all right? Whoever killed him could still be in the area. You might be in danger. Is anyone with you?"

She shook her head, trying to clear away the image in front of her. "No, I'm alone. I'm in the forest behind the center, on the far right side. Take the path named Tranquility and about halfway down it you'll see a path that leads to the right. It's a shortcut. I'll wait for you."

"All right. Stay there. You're probably safe. I imagine whoever did it is gone by now. I need to call Rich. Don't touch Scott or anything else."

She continued to look at Scott, trying to understand why anyone would want to kill him. No one came to mind. All she could think about was how everyone loved and respected the man. A few minutes later, she heard footsteps behind her and whirled around. "Oh Mike, I'm so glad you're here." She ran over to him and tearfully threw her arms around him.

"Kelly, it's okay. I'm here." He held her closely, gently stroking her back. Soon, he could feel her body stop shaking. "Stay here," he said, releasing her and walking over to Scott's body. He was quiet for several minutes and then he turned back to her. "Kelly, you were right. He's dead and it's an obvious homicide."

They heard footsteps and saw Mike's chief deputy sheriff, Rich, striding towards them, gun drawn. Several students were following him. "Rich, secure the area as an active crime scene and call the coroner. Also, you need to alert our crime scene investigators and have them come out here as soon as possible."

"Step back, everyone," Rich said. He took his phone out of its holster and made the calls Mike had requested. A large man pushed through the quickly gathering crowd and ran past Mike and Rich. He stopped and stared at Scott's body lying on the forest floor.

Mike walked over to him and put his hand on the man's arm. "Don't touch the body. This is now a crime scene. I'm going to have to ask you to leave."

"That's my brother and I'm not leaving him! What happened?" he screamed. "Who did this?" He fell to the ground, sobbing, and put his arms around Scott's immobile body.

Kelly had met Scott's brother, Luke Monroe, on several prior occasions and had taken a couple of yoga classes from him. She walked over to where Luke was lying prostrate on the ground. "I'm so sorry. I was coming back from the walking meditation and took a shortcut. At first when I saw Scott's beard I thought it was a black bear." She began to cry again and was so overcome with emotion she couldn't speak.

Mike had been on his phone while Kelly spoke to Luke. He turned to face what had quickly become a crowd of people. "I want each one of you to remain here. My deputy and I need to talk to you. We'll be with you shortly. While you're waiting, try to think if you saw or heard anything unusual." He turned to Kelly. "I'll begin with you. I want you to tell me everything you saw and heard from the moment you drove up the road leading to the Center."

She recounted everything to him. "Kelly, were there any unusual people in the class? Was there anything different during the class or did you notice something or hear anything when you were out here walking?"

"This is my first class at the Center in a couple of months, so I really don't know much. I recognized some familiar faces from when I've taken workshops and classes here over the years, but that's about it. As for when I was walking in the forest, I didn't see or hear anything unusual. I sure didn't hear anything that sounded like a gunshot."

Mike turned to Luke. "I'll need to talk to you at length. I recall Kelly telling me that you moved here from the East Coast and were helping Scott run the Center. I'd like you to try and think of anyone who might have a motive for killing your brother. I know this is terribly painful for you, but tell me everything that comes to you, no matter how trivial you may think it is. I'll get back to you later.

"Rich, I've called Dave and Joe. I told them to get to the Center as fast as they could. I'll start interviewing these people here, but in the meantime, I want you to go back to the Center and put the people who are there in one room. When Dave and Joe get here they can interview them, then I need you to come back here and help me with these people. Dave and Joe should be here within minutes. Kelly, you can go home now. Do you think you can drive?"

"Yes," she said in a shaky voice. She walked over to Luke. "Your brother was one of the finest men I've ever known. I promise you we'll find out who did this." She looked up at Mike and noticed him shaking his head when she said "we." He wasn't very happy with her involvement in his cases. That had been the only disturbing element in their otherwise perfect relationship. She didn't know how she was going to find out who killed Scott, only that she would. She wished she could have stayed and listened to what everyone had to say, but she knew that for now, Mike wanted her to leave. She was already planning on finding a way to talk to Luke tomorrow without offending Mike or making it look like she was once again getting involved in one of his cases.

CHAPTER FOUR

Rich felt the tension and unrest as soon as he opened the front door of the Retreat Center. The crowd of men and women couldn't figure out why there were two sheriff's cars in the Center's parking lot. He heard snippets of conversations indicating that rumors were being born. Within minutes the sound of sirens was heard and soon blue and red flashing lights filled the lot. Dave and Joe threw open the doors of their patrol cars and raced up the steps to the front door.

Students from the different classes held at the Center, people taking part in the residential training program, and workers at the Center were all talking to one another, trying to find out what happened. The rumor that Zen Master Scott was dead was circulating like wildfire, but everyone hoped it was only that, an unfounded rumor. They'd gravitated toward the large yoga room and Rich sequestered them in it. He saw Dave and Joe in the hallway when they entered the building.

"Dave, Joe, stay where you are, there in the hallway." He turned to the crowd of concerned people gathered in the room. "I'm sorry to confirm what you may have heard, that Zen Master Scott was killed earlier..." He was interrupted by a number of people asking him who had done it, when it had happened, how it had been done, and every other question that popped into their minds. Several people began crying, some openly sobbing, others silently weeping. Zen Master Scott was beloved by all of them.

Rich continued, "There are two officers out in the hall who will be interviewing you shortly. If you think of anything you may have seen or heard which seemed unusual, please tell them. They'll want to know where you were between 3:00 p.m. and 3:20 p.m. this afternoon. Evidently Mr. Monroe was killed sometime during that time frame. He was in this room teaching a yoga class until 3:00 p.m. when he took the class into the forest for a walking meditation. His body was found by one of the students at 3:20 p.m., so it's a pretty safe guess to say he was killed sometime between 3:00 p.m. and 3:20 p.m. Please cooperate fully with these officers. Finding the killer of Scott Monroe is our primary concern. I'm returning to the scene of the murder to interview the students who gathered there following the walking meditation."

He walked out of the room and into the hall. "Dave, Joe, the people in that room all have something to do with the Center. Some are students who take classes here and others live on the property, either working here or taking part in the residential training program. I understand there are some priests and nuns who live on the property, probably in one of the other buildings, and Mike and I will interview them. Anyway, I want you to find out where each of these people was between 3:00 p.m. and 3:20 p.m. this afternoon as well as any other relevant information you can find out from them. When you're finished, give Mike or me a call. If you're comfortable releasing them, go ahead, but make sure you have contact information for each of them. If there's anything you think we need to know, don't hesitate to call us. Talk to you later."

*****

Well, I guess he should have taken me up on my offer to come to my apartment. If I can't have him, I'm glad no one else can either. He may have said he was celibate, but I never believed him. Guess now I'll never find out. He was the only person beside my mother who ever really cared for me. I remember when he told me I had pretty feet, just like she used to tell me. I wonder if I'll miss him as much as I miss her.

CHAPTER FIVE

Kelly quietly got out of bed and tiptoed out of the bedroom. She didn't want to wake up Mike. He'd called her the evening before, telling her he wouldn't be home for several hours and not to wait up for him. He'd been tied up at the Center interviewing people and then he had to go to his office to do the necessary paperwork on the case. She let Rebel, the guard dog she'd had for several years, and Lady, her new Labrador retriever puppy, out the back door, and made some coffee.

I need to talk to Luke. He and Scott were close, plus he was helping Scott run the Center. He must know something. Think I'll go to the coffee shop, make a casserole, and take it out to the Center and give it to him. He can either eat it today or freeze it and have it later.

She opened the door and let the dogs back in. Lady stayed next to Rebel, imitating whatever he did. The drug agent who had trained Rebel and then was killed in the line of duty had made sure Rebel was housebroken, stayed off of the furniture, and didn't chew on non-doggy treats. Lady was so enamored of her "big brother," she wanted to be just like him. Fortunately, he was a very good role model for the growing little bundle of fur to follow. At four months old, she was stepping out of puppyhood. She slept next to Rebel, ate next to him, and accompanied him when he patrolled the property to make sure Kelly was safe. Privately Kelly thought Lady was as observant as Rebel. She'd noticed in the short time she'd had Lady that she was becoming as devoted to her as Rebel had once been. She was pretty sure that one of the reasons Mike had gotten Lady for her was because Rebel was gradually switching his loyalty from Kelly to Mike.

"Rebel, you stay here with Mike. Lady, come. We're going to the coffee shop." She wrote a note to Mike telling him she was going to the coffee shop so she could get ready for the coming week.

Several hours later she headed south along the coast thinking how typical the day was for January – drizzly and cloudy. *No wonder the grapes grow so well at the White Cloud Retreat Center. It's always misty and cloudy there. Then a little sun comes out to help ripen the grapes and voila, you have perfect weather for a killer pinot noir wine. And the Center definitely makes a killer pinot noir!*

She pulled into the parking lot of the Retreat Center and told Lady to stay. She noticed that Lady positioned herself in the exact spot Rebel always occupied when she left him in the minivan – standing on the passenger seat until she returned, protecting the turf. As she walked up the steps to the front door of the Center, she saw a piece of white paper tacked to the door with the words "Classes Cancelled All Week. Will Resume on Saturday" written on it.

Kelly knocked on the door. Usually students simply opened the door, walked into the center, and went to the room where their class was going to be held. When no one answered, she knocked again. There was still no answer. She tried the door knob and it opened easily. She took a tentative step into the hallway and didn't see anyone. She was debating what to do next when a tall, athletic looking man wearing yoga pants and a T-shirt walked up to her. "May I help you?" he asked.

"Yes. My name is Kelly Connor and I'm here to see Luke Monroe. Is he available?"

"He's in the office, looking over some papers. I don't think he's in the mood for visitors, but I can ask him, if you'd like."

"Please. I was the one who discovered his brother's body yesterday. I've come to give my condolences and I brought him some food."

"I'll go ask him, but don't be disappointed if the answer is no."

"I understand."

He returned a few minutes later. "Luke said he could talk to you for a few minutes. Please follow me."

She walked into the large room which prior to Scott's death, had served as his combination office and study. Bookcases filled with books lined the walls. A large roll-top oak desk was situated in front of the windows, providing an excellent view of the vineyard and the ocean beyond. Luke Monroe was sitting behind the desk. He looked up from a file he was reading and greeted her.

"Hello, Kelly. I know my brother was a friend of yours. Scott's death must be hard on you as well. Please, sit down."

He turned to the young man who had escorted her into the room. "Blaine, I'd appreciate it if you would handle any other calls or people who stop by for the rest of the day. If it's something you can't handle, ask Zeb to take care of it. Thanks." He turned back to Kelly. "Zeb's the second priest in charge after Scott. He's taking care of the day-to-day matters relating to the Center."

"I just want to tell you again how sorry I am about the loss of your brother. I can't understand why anyone would want to kill him. I considered Scott to be a good friend. I'm getting married in a few weeks and he told me if my Catholic priest couldn't marry us because my fiancé's divorced, he'd be happy to perform the ceremony. It was a very kind and thoughtful gesture for him to make and I really appreciated it."

Luke wiped a tear away from his eyes. "I'm sorry. As much as I've cried in the last twenty-four hours, I didn't think I had any more tears left. It seems surreal and although Scott and I were estranged for a number of years, in the last year we really became close. It was a brother thing, I guess. He couldn't understand why I was so intent on following the gods of commercialism and I couldn't understand why he was following the teachings of the Eastern ways. What a stupid waste of time for both of us! And now he's gone." He shook his head from side to side as if that would get rid of the grief he was feeling.

"I know it may be premature, but are you planning on running the White Cloud Retreat Center yourself or will you be asking some other Zen priest like Zeb to assume the role of Master?"

"I don't know. I've been a Zen student for a few years and although Scott was a Zen Master, the Center has never been strictly a Zen Center. By that I mean all kinds of different beliefs were studied here, not just Zen Buddhism. Scott embraced all beliefs. I could run the Center as a non-denominational Center, but what most people don't know is that Scott actually ordained me recently as a Zen priest.

"He conducted a very simple ceremony called a Tokudo for me. It was attended by only the nuns and priests who are in residence here. I took some vows and agreed to devote my life to Buddhism. He chanted a few verses from the Buddhist texts and gave me some robes and food bowls.

"The bowls he gave me were strictly ceremonial. In some countries, even today, the monks leave their monasteries at dawn with their bowls and the villagers put food in them. According to tradition, giving food to the monks is considered a way of gaining merit. In some monasteries a monk isn't allowed to consume food after midday and isn't allowed to store food overnight. The monk is expected to live on whatever's offered by the villagers, that's why so many monks are vegetarians. That was it."

"You're kidding! I thought you had to do a lot more than that to become a Zen priest."

"No. Some ceremonies are very elaborate and others are almost dirt simple. Knowing Scott, you can imagine he'd go for the dirt simple, so theoretically I'm a Zen Buddhist priest. I became a vegetarian after I'd been here at the Center for a few weeks. The cook here is so good that I've never missed not eating meat. I'm divorced, so although I haven't been celibate, I could be, even though that's not a prerequisite to being a Zen priest. Scott certainly took his vow of celibacy seriously, probably to the regret of some of our female students. Drinking wine isn't a problem, although there are a couple of winemakers in the area who would love to see the Center no longer produce wine. I've heard rumors they're pretty jealous of our success. I'm not surprised to hear that given how good the Center's wines are and their reputation for excellence in the wine industry.

"Luke, let's talk for a minute about who might have killed Scott and why. What about religious zealots? Cedar Bay is a small town and this whole area is pretty conservative. Did Scott ever mention that someone may not have been happy that the Retreat Center was here? It's certainly not a bastion of old line Christian thinking."

"Kelly, I've racked my brain trying to come up with who might have had some motive for wanting to kill Scott and I haven't come up with an answer. Sure, some wacko could be responsible, but they would have had to have taken part in the walking meditation or else laid in wait for Scott in the forest. The forest area that surrounds the Center is pretty impenetrable. Neither of those options seems to make a lot of sense."

"Well, I'm sure this is a distasteful thought, but could it have been someone who's a resident here at the Center?"

"It could be anybody, but the nuns and priests here loved him. And why would someone come here to study with him and then kill him? That doesn't make any sense either."

"I agree. I don't want to take up any more of your time, but here's a casserole I made for you. You can freeze it or eat it right away and fortunately, it doesn't have any meat in it!"

"Thank you very much, Kelly. My brother mentioned that you were very involved in helping solve a couple of murders which happened recently in the local area. How about you? Do you have any thoughts as to who might have killed Scott?"

"I wish I did. If something comes to mind, I'll call you. To change the subject, and I know you haven't had much time to think about it, but have you made a decision regarding a service for Scott?"

"Yes. Zeb and I met this morning. It's traditional for Buddhists to be cremated upon their death. That's what we're going to do. Zeb and I will conduct a simple ceremony here at the Center Thursday afternoon he's been cremated. Anyone is welcome to come."

"Luke, I've never been to a Buddhist funeral service. What's expected? I'd very much like to come."

"Nothing is expected. Often mourners will bring offerings of flowers or fruit. Incense will be burned and usually the mourners wear white. We're planning on doing it Thursday from 4:00 p.m. to 6:00 p.m. You're more than welcome to come. In fact, I hope a lot of people from Cedar Bay come. I know that Scott believed death is simply a transition from one form of life to another, but even though I've taken the vows of Zen Buddhism, I'm struggling with that concept at the moment. Seems like there's a lot of finality in death when you can't talk to the person anymore."

Kelly stood up and walked over to him, putting her hand on his arm. "Luke, I know a lot of people are going to depend on you in the next few weeks, but if you ever want to talk to someone, I've got a big ear and a strong shoulder to cry on. I'd consider it an honor if you would."

"Thanks for the offer, but I hope I won't have to take you up on it. I'm curious how you and Scott came to be friends. When did you meet Scott? As soon as he bought the property or later?"

"I think it was several months afterwards. He came to the coffee shop one day and we talked about food and wine and the Center. I told him I wasn't getting any younger and I was often tired and tense after spending most of the day on my feet. He suggested I come to the Center and take a yoga and meditation class. I took a number of classes as well as some workshops and I always felt better afterwards, so it was after the Center had been operating for a few months that I first met him."

"I just thought of something. It's probably nothing, but last week he mentioned he'd been getting phone calls. As soon as he answered, whoever was on the line hung up. We have a telephone number for the Center, but these hang-up calls went to his cell phone. He thought it was just some wacko. Now I wonder."

"Where's his cell phone?"

"I gave it to Sheriff Mike when he talked to me yesterday."

"I'll be seeing Mike when I leave here and I'll mention it to him. It's probably nothing, but he should know about it."

"I agree. Thanks again for coming, Kelly, and let's stay in touch."

"Well, if I don't hear from you this week, I'll see you Thursday afternoon at Scott's service."

She walked out to where Lady was standing in the minivan, waiting for her safe return. "Okay, Lady, back seat." Lady turned and jumped into the back seat, just as Rebel had shown her.

If I didn't know better, I'd think these two dogs are telepathic. Then again maybe they are and I don't know any better.

CHAPTER SIX

The two brothers sat quietly in the office of Pellino Brothers Vineyard while one of them, Dante, dialed the special telephone number they'd been told to use if they ever needed to privately contact Angelo Rossi at his office in Chicago.

"Hello. Rossi Exports and Imports. May I help you?" the young female voice asked.

"Yes, my name is Dante Pellino and I'm calling from the Pellino Brothers Vineyard in Oregon. Mr. Rossi gave me this number to call if I ever needed to talk with him about a private business matter. May I speak with him, please?"

"He's pretty busy right now. I don't know if he can take your call, but since you're calling on his preferred line, I'm pretty sure he'll want to talk to you. We don't get many calls on this line. I'll put you on hold."

"Hello, Dante," a man with a strong Italian accent said moments later. "Nice to hear from you. How are you and your brother doing with my special vineyard out there in Oregon?"

"We're doing fine, Mr. Rossi. I'm calling from the vineyard and I have my brother, Luca, listening in on the speaker phone. You told us to never call you at this number unless there was a major problem

21

here at the vineyard that we couldn't handle. Unfortunately, a serious situation has developed and we need your help and advice.

"Not a problem, boys. I'm glad you called. You know I have five million dollars of the Family's money tied up in that vineyard and I don't want anything to go wrong. That's why I sent the two of you out to Oregon from Chicago to run it for me and protect the Family's investment. All the phony paperwork that's been filed with the state shows that the two of you are the sole and exclusive legal owners of the vineyard. Neither I nor any of the Family members are shown as part owners of the business. That's the way we want it in case the FBI ever comes after our assets. Given the popularity of wine in today's market and the huge increase in wine sales and prices, we're convinced there are millions of dollars to be made in the wine business. We want to be in on the ground floor of it so we can make that kind money. Plus, it's a completely legitimate business that helps us unload some of the excess cash we generate from our business operations here in Chicago, if you know what I mean. Now what's this problem you referred to that's so important you had to call me on my special phone line?"

"Well, this is the situation, Mr. Rossi. For the past few years the production results here at Pellino Brothers Vineyard have far exceed our expectations. The total number of cases of wine we've been able to produce and bottle per acre of vines is way above the state and regional average. We've been able to do this because we've been using a lot of pesticides and herbicides that have been banned for use by the Environmental Protection Agency. The EPA claims these chemicals can cause cancer and pollute the ground water. Also, one of the banned herbicides we use, called Dead Bang, can cause a disease in grape vines called brown leaf spot. If any of this particular herbicide comes in contact with the leaves on the grape vines, the leaves turn brown and the vine eventually dies. I'm sure you're aware that your company has been secretly providing those chemicals for us to use for a number of years. In fact Rossi Trucking Company delivered thirty fifty-five gallon drums to us just last week. I don't know how you get the stuff, but I'll tell you this, it works like a miracle and it's the main reason the vineyard is doing so well.

"Here's the problem we wanted to discuss with you, Mr. Rossi. There's another vineyard located across the road from our vineyard called White Cloud Vineyard. It's owned by some Eastern spiritual guy who teaches Zen Buddhist and yoga stuff to people who come to classes at a Retreat Center located in his vineyard. He goes by the name of Zen Master Scott Monroe. He came to our place last week and accused us of using Dead Bang to control the weeds in our vineyard. He claimed it drifted across the road and contaminated his vineyard, which, by the way, is a fully organic vineyard. He doesn't allow the use of any type of herbicide, pesticide, or fertilizer on his property. Naturally, we denied using Dead Bang and told him his problems must be coming from some other source.

"We didn't tell him that we'd sprayed our entire vineyard with Dead Bang about a week before this guy Scott showed up to complain. When we apply it we're very careful to make sure it doesn't come in contact with any of our vines. However, it was very windy on the day we sprayed Dead Bang on the weeds in our vineyard and I suppose some of it could have been carried by the prevailing winds over onto his property and contaminated his vines. He said some of his leaves had brown leaf spot on them and it must have come from our vineyard because the only thing that could cause brown leaf spot on his vines was Dead Bang. He told us that in ten days he was going to report us to the Oregon Depart of Agriculture for using Dead Bang unless we provided him with positive proof that we've destroyed any and all banned chemicals located on the property. If he reports us as he's threatened to do and the State officials do tests and confirm that we've been using illegal chemicals, they can shut down our vineyard operations without even having to get a Court Order. If that happens, we won't be allowed to harvest any grapes from the vines in our vineyard for a minimum of three years and perhaps even longer. It will put us out of business.

"The reason Luca and I are calling you is to see if there's any way you can help us stop this guy from reporting us to the state agricultural officials. I don't know, maybe some kind of a financial payoff might work, but from what I hear, the Retreat Center is rolling in money."

"I'm glad you boys called. You're right. It does sound like it could be a real problem. Let me do this. I have a business associate who works for me by the name of Guido who has special ways of resolving business disputes like this one. I'll have him fly out to Portland tonight. He can rent a car and be at your vineyard sometime early tomorrow morning. Be on the lookout for him. I'll give him some special instructions on how to deal with the problem. I want you to cooperate with him and do whatever he asks you to do. Got it?"

"Yes, thanks, Mr. Rossi. We knew you could help us make this problem go away."

CHAPTER SEVEN

"We're home," Kelly said in a loud voice as she and Lady walked through the door. Rebel walked over to Lady and sniffed her, making sure she hadn't been mistakenly given a treat that had been meant for him.

"Missed you, Babe. I got home late last night and slept in this morning. Thanks for the note," he said. "That's a long time to spend at the coffee shop on a Sunday."

"Yeah, well I had a lot to do. What with Scott's murder, we both know it will be a zoo there tomorrow. You know how people love to come to the coffee shop to gossip when something out of the ordinary happens in Cedar Bay, and Scott's death definitely qualifies as out of the ordinary. We'll probably be jammed from the time we open until we close. I did as much as I could ahead of time. Charlie's great as a fry cook, but I thought we might need some extra things if tomorrow's going to be anything like the day after Amber's death and Jeff's death. Profitable yes, but also very exhausting," she said, taking off her coat and putting it in the hall closet. "I haven't had a chance to talk to you yet about Scott's murder. Do you have any suspects?"

"No, not yet. This has to be one of the most frustrating cases I've ever been involved in. Rich and I interviewed everyone who was at the crime scene as well as the priests and nuns who live at the Center. Dave and Joe interviewed the rest of the people who were at the Retreat Center and there wasn't a single person who gave any of us a clue or helped us with the case in any way. It appears that Scott was universally liked, loved, respected, and idolized. I hope when I go people will be that adoring of me, but given my line of work, I doubt if that will happen."

"If it's any consolation, I'll promise to be that adoring."

"Thanks, Sweetheart, I needed that. Now that we have that out of the way, what's for dinner?"

"A vegetarian casserole. Don't stick your nose up like that. It will be very healthy for you and as much stress as you're under, you don't need to eat a lot of heavy, meaty dishes. They're not good for you. Anyway, I made one for Luke Monroe and took it to him this afternoon to express my condolences. Since I was already making one, I decided to make two, so we could have one tonight." She turned away from Mike, pretty sure that the disapproving expression on his face was intended for her.

"You made a casserole for Luke, took it out to him, and expressed your condolences. How very nice of you. Kelly, how many times do we have to have this conversation? You are not the sheriff. You are not supposed to try and solve my cases. I'm the sheriff and the cases are mine. I admit that you were very lucky when you got involved in Amber and Jeff's murders and helped solve them, but please stay out of this investigation. Scott was a guy who was loved by everyone and as of this moment, there's not even one viable suspect. Do we have an understanding regarding this case?" he asked in a very low, stern voice.

"Of course we do," she said, mentally crossing her fingers behind her back, "but what about the person who kept calling him on his cell phone and then hanging up? I'd think whoever did that might qualify as a suspect."

"What are you talking about?"

She told him about the conversation she'd had with Luke. "And what about the fact that a lot of women found Scott pretty desirable, even though he told me he was celibate. Might want to follow up and see if any of them was a little too attracted to him and became frustrated when their adoration wasn't being returned. And what about the estrangement between him and his brother? Did you know about that?"

"All right, I give. Sit down and tell me everything you've learned."

After she'd finished relating her conversation with Luke, Mike called his deputy. "Rich, first thing in the morning I want you to call the Retreat Center and find out from Scott's brother what phone company Scott used as a service provider for his cell phone. Once you've found that out, call the company and tell them we need to have a record of all the incoming calls on his cell phone for the past month. I put his phone in the evidence locker last night. You've got a key. Evidently Scott had a lot of hang-up calls recently. It's a long shot, but considering we don't have anything else to go on at this point, we need to try it. I also want you to find out from his brother, Luke, where the two of them grew up. Get as much early childhood and family background information as you can from him."

He was quiet while he listened to Rich. "I think I need to look into Scott's background. That's always a good place to start. Maybe somebody from his hometown knows something." He ran his hand over his face in frustration. "Right now we're just taking potshots at anything that moves, looking for something. See you tomorrow," he said as he ended the call.

"Well Miss Crime Solver," he said turning towards Kelly with a smile on his face, "do you have any more brilliant thoughts regarding my case? And I almost forgot. I got about ten hang-up calls today. Was that you?"

"Of course not. You know I'd leave a message. Probably somebody kept plugging in the wrong number. Don't be nasty, but yes, now that you mention it, I do have a few thoughts. Many people think Zen is some kind of a weird Eastern religion and generally speaking, they don't trust Eastern religions or practices. There's a church group that comes to the coffee shop every Tuesday at lunchtime after their weekly Bible study meeting. They're pretty much fire and brimstone Christian believers. I wonder if they'd have any thoughts on who might hate a Zen Master enough to kill him."

"I'd like to tell you not to get involved. I'd like you to stick to what you know best, cooking and yes, there are a lot of things I'd like you to do and not do, but I know that's not going to happen. I'm sure you're already thinking about the Tuesday group and what you might find out from them. I'm not happy about you interfering, but yes, I would like to know what you find out."

"Got it, Sheriff. You'll be the first to know and maybe if we shared whatever information either of us gets, we could solve this case faster."

"We, and I repeat the word we, are not going to solve this case. I am going to solve this case. If you know something that might help me solve my case, I would appreciate it. Is that understood?"

"Yes, sir," she said sarcastically. "Since that's understood, time to eat. By the way, the wedding's less than three weeks away. A little less heavy food might be good for both of us. Remember, all eyes will be on us."

You're wrong, he thought. *All eyes will be on you, not on a middle-aged man with a receding hairline who carries about ten pounds too many on his body. They'll be looking at your beautiful black hair, porcelain–like complexion, and a figure women twenty years your junior would kill for. No, Kelly, I'm simply an addendum to you, but a mighty happy addendum. Just be careful this time if you feel compelled to do a little investigating on your own. Now that I've found you, I don't want to lose you!*

*****

The man dressed in loose yoga pants, a sweater, and a jacket, looked around the vineyard where he was standing and at the White Cloud Retreat Center located a short distance away. Guess Scott's sorry now he got mad at me for pruning the vines a little shorter than he liked. The dumb vines will grow just fine no matter how I prune them. Probably not many vines where he is now, so he'll just have to find something else to criticize. He had to go. There was no way I was going to be the Zen Master as long as he stayed here. It's a good thing I don't take my medications any more. Zen Masters probably shouldn't be taking anti-psychotic medications. I never needed that stuff anyway. Rest In Peace Mr. Big Shot Zen Master.

CHAPTER EIGHT

Early Monday morning, Kelly dressed in her usual coffee shop attire of jeans and a red T-shirt with the words, Kelly's Koffee Shop, emblazoned in white on it, and took her keys from the rack near the front door. She motioned for Lady to come with her. For the last few weeks when Kelly left early in the morning for the coffee shop, Rebel had opted to stay at the house with Mike. Mike woke up a couple of hours after Kelly left and took Rebel with him to the sheriff's office. Rebel was getting older and didn't mind getting the extra few hours of sleep.

She parked her minivan in the lot adjacent to the pier and opened the door for Lady who immediately ran down the pier to where Madison, Charlie, and Roxie were waiting for Kelly to open up the coffee shop. Each of them reached down to give the growing puppy an ear scratch. The three of them were well trained as Rebel had let it be known over the years exactly what dogs like. Kelly waved to them, silently giving thanks to the coffee house gods for sending these loyal employees her way.

Her grandparents had started selling coffee and sweet rolls out of a small little building on the pier many years before she was born. At the time, the lumber industry was flourishing in the area and most of their customers had been lumbermen. It wasn't long before they started requesting different kinds of food and the little coffee shop had expanded several times over the years, becoming an institution in the small town. At some point, almost everyone in Cedar Bay had passed through the front door of Kelly's Koffee Shop. When Kelly's grandparents passed away, Kelly's parents had taken over the coffee shop and named it Kelly's Koffee Shop in honor of their daughter. When they retired, Kelly and her husband, Mark, ran it, however, Mark died at a very early age from a rare type of cancer. Since then, the coffee shop had supported Kelly and her children, Julia and Cash. It was open for breakfast and lunch Monday through Friday. On any day of the week a number of the regulars would be there as well as tourists who were exploring the Oregon coast.

Kelly was certain that a lot of the people who ate at the coffee shop came because of Roxie. She'd been with Kelly for over ten years and was one of those people who made you feel good by just being around them. Roxie not only knew everybody by name and everything about them, but she really cared about them. You always felt better after talking to Roxie.

Charlie was the son of Chief Many Trees and lived on the Indian reservation just outside of town. Even though he was surly and deeply suspicious of anything relating to the government because of the harm he felt it had done to his tribe, he was a very valued employee. Kelly made the signature coffee shop casseroles and a lot of the other things, but Charlie was the one responsible for the short orders and Kelly was always amazed by how many orders he could juggle and prepare at the same time. The newest addition to the coffee shop staff was Madison, who had replaced Amber after she'd been murdered. Madison's life had taken a turn for the better when her father stopped drinking and she'd started attending cosmetology school in Sunset Bay after she graduated from high school. Kelly knew she only had a few more months until she'd have to replace Madison at the coffee shop. Wanda, the owner of the town beauty parlor, planned on hiring Madison full-time as soon as she received her license. She was already interning at Wanda's beauty parlor after Kelly's closed for the day at 2:00 p.m.

"Morning, everyone. How was your weekend?" Kelly asked.

"Probably not half as exciting as yours was," Charlie said. "Rumor around town is that you're the one who discovered the Zen Master's body. Any truth to it?"

"I should know by now that nothing happens in this town without everyone knowing about it, but it still amazes me how fast word travels. Yes, I discovered Scott's body. You may have heard he was shot. That's all I know. Mike's working on the case, but so far he doesn't seem to have any suspects in mind. The Center is having a service for Scott Thursday afternoon from 4:00 p.m. to 6:00 p.m., if any of you are interested in attending."

"You know it's funny," Roxie said. "I don't remember ever hearing about a murder in Cedar Bay before Amber's, and now with Jeff and Scott, that makes three in just a few short months. Wonder if the town has bad juju or something."

Kelly flipped the light switch on as the four of them entered the coffee shop. "Don't know about that, but I do know we're probably going to be pretty busy today. People always seem to come to find out all the latest rumors when something happens around here. I came in yesterday and made some things, but I need the three of you to hustle because there's a good chance we'll have some early birds this morning. Madison, I'd like you to turn the ovens on right away. Charlie, I bought a lot of sausage. On cold wet days like today, people love to order biscuits and sausage gravy. Think it's a comfort food thing. Anyway, I made the biscuits yesterday. You can start the gravy."

Shortly after 7:00 a.m., the normal opening time for the coffee shop, it was already filled with curiosity seekers. A number of the townspeople had taken workshops and classes at the Retreat Center or had bought some of their wine. Scott was very much liked and everyone who knew him felt a personal loss. Kelly, Roxie, and Charlie worked nonstop. Madison had to leave at 9:00 to attend her cosmetology classes, but promised to return right after they ended.

Promptly at noon, just as he did every day of the workday week, Doc walked into the coffee shop with the yellow lab Kelly had given him. Doc stopped to give Lady an ear scratch and Lucky, Doc's dog, sniffed her and wagged his tail. "Doc, let me wipe this table down and you can sit here."

He slid into the booth and wound Lucky's leash around the back of a nearby chair. "Doc, I'm surprised to see Lucky on a leash. Thought you were going to train him to do everything off leash."

"I have, but the one place I don't want to create a disturbance is here at your coffee shop. Between the plates, coffee cups, glasses, and everything else, you've got a lot of breakable stuff in here. He still gets distracted and I don't want to be responsible for Madison or Roxie having an accident or even worse, some customer who's not used to dogs, panicking, and spooking him. Could be a disaster."

"Thanks. That I don't need. I've just gotten Lady to the point where I can keep her off leash while she's here at the coffee shop with me. She knows her place is on her bed by the cash register. I try to keep her out of the kitchen because I'm not real sure if it's against the Oregon Health Department's rules and I really don't want to find out. It's one of those, 'if it ain't broke, don't fix it' things."

"I understand. I don't think I've ever seen a dog that young be so good off leash. Are you doing something special? I thought I was pretty good with dogs, but I think you have me beat by a long shot."

"Jackie Lewis, the owner of the kennel where I got Lady, told me that Lady was probably the smartest dog she'd ever had at her kennel. Maybe that has something to do with it, or then again, maybe she just watches Rebel and tries to do everything exactly like he does."

"Well, whatever it is, it's working. I'm starving. What do you recommend on today's menu?"

"That's easy. Biscuits and sausage gravy. I made the biscuits and Charlie makes the best sausage gravy I've ever had. Can't be beat on a gloomy January day like today."

"You've sold me. I heard about Scott and I'm really sorry. I liked him a lot. He was one of my first patients at the clinic after I got my

Oregon medical license. I'm going to miss him. It's hard to believe someone would want to kill him. I can't imagine why. I also heard you were the one who found him. Is that right?"

"That I did and like you, I can't believe anyone would want to kill him. I can't even begin to think what the motive might have been. I've never heard anyone say a bad word about him. Did he ever say anything to you? Since he's deceased, you wouldn't be violating a patient's confidence by telling me anything you might know about him."

"As soon as I heard about it, I replayed our past conversations in my mind. He was actually in pretty good health. He came to me because he had a nasty laceration on his arm from one of those rose bushes they have at the end of each row of grapevines out at the Center. It had happened a few days before he came to see me. I remember asking him why there was a rose bush in a vineyard, since it seemed like a strange place for one to be. He told me rose bushes showed problems with mildew and other plant diseases long before they showed up on the grapevines themselves. I thought that was an interesting self-help way to keep the vines healthy. I guess it was part of his being an organic vineyard owner. Anyway, the cut just needed a couple of stitches and he was fine after that. He came back for a follow-up visit two weeks later and he was perfectly healed."

"I'm not surprised he didn't seek medical help right away. From everything I know about him he led about as healthful a life as anyone could. He was a little overweight, but I doubt if he visited a doctor very often."

"That's true, but I do remember he was pretty upset when he came back for his follow-up visit. He mentioned that being the head of a Center like his had its share of problems. Evidently he'd had some harsh words with one of the men in the residential training program at the Center. They're required to work in the vineyards as part of the program and this particular man pruned the vines shorter than Scott wanted them to be. Scott was still angry about it because he was afraid the vines might not bear fruit in the next growing season due to the man's improper pruning.

"He also mentioned that a couple of the wine growers from the region would love it if his White Cloud Pinot Noir didn't sell as well as it does now. He said they barely spoke to him at the Oregon Wine Festival he attended last year because the Center's wine was getting far better ratings than theirs. They told him their vineyard was a family business that was run for profit and it was unfair for a non-profit like White Cloud Center to compete with them. They claimed he could eventually put them out of business. Why do you ask?"

"I'm looking for anything that might tell us why he was killed. I don't know much about the wine industry, but maybe his death has something to do with it. Remember any names?"

"Nope. Just that they were local. You could probably…whoops! Slip of the tongue on my part. Actually, Mike could probably find out on the Internet who grows pinot noir grapes locally. Shouldn't be too hard to do. Better yet, he could ask Jesse, the owner of The Crush, the local wine store here in Cedar Bay. I'll bet he'd know."

"Thanks, Doc, I'll be sure and tell Mike," she said, mentally crossing her fingers behind her back. "Just sit there and relax and I'll have your order ready in no time."

"Kelly, I know it's none of my business, but you do remember the promises I've heard you make to Mike about not helping him with his cases. Right?"

"Absolutely, Doc. Not a problem."

Sorry, Doc. Mike doesn't like to admit it, but he needs my help. Anyway, where would you be if I hadn't been responsible for suggesting you help out at the clinic and you met Liz? And don't forget I gave Lucky to you as a congratulatory gift when you found out you'd been reinstated by the California Medical Board. And I believed you when you told me you had nothing to do with Amber's death. If it wasn't for me, you might still be a suspect in Amber's death.

As she walked into the kitchen to get Doc's order, she was already making plans in her mind to go to The Crush and talk to Jesse as soon as she closed up the coffee shop that afternoon.

CHAPTER NINE

When Kelly returned and placed the heaping plate of biscuits and sausage gravy in front of him, Doc said, "Looks like there might be a slight break in the action. Got something else I'd like to run by you."

"Sure, Doc. I can spare a few minutes. Just let me tell Roxie to cover for me." In a few moments she returned and sat across from him. "What is it?"

"Well, remember how I told you about my divorce and having two sons that I hadn't seen since I left California?"

"Yes, I remember. I thought it was a very sad situation and yet, from what you told me, your wife and the boys didn't want anything to do with you after you were found liable in that civil lawsuit regarding the young woman you performed the abortion on."

"I've wanted to pick up the phone a million times and call the boys, but I never did. I figured the boys didn't need a dad in their lives who'd been found liable in court for civil damages and whose medical license had been revoked by the California State Medical Board. No, I figured they were better off without me, but once I was reinstated, I started thinking about them a lot. I wondered if they knew I was practicing medicine again. I also wondered whatever happened to the three million dollar judgment that was entered against me. The parents of the young girl who died were the ones who sued me and obtained the judgment. When they were killed in an airplane accident, the right to collect the judgment against me passed to their son, the brother of the young girl who died.

"Liz and I talked about it a lot and she finally convinced me to call my attorney and see if he knew what had happened. It turns out he'd tried to reach me to tell me that the girl's brother was giving up his attempts to find me and collect the judgment. Evidently he married a doctor and she convinced him that I wasn't negligent in his sister's death. He said the woman told the young man that there are things in medicine that just happen and they can't be explained. She'd been curious about the case and had read all of the evidence. She convinced him, regardless of the jury's decision, that I wasn't to blame for his sister's death. The attorney told me the brother had taken the necessary steps to dismiss the case."

"Doc, that's wonderful news! I guess it means you can get in touch with your sons now that no one is trying to find you."

"That's exactly what it means. Once Liz heard about it, she had me on the phone with them within the hour and wouldn't let me hang up. It wasn't a particularly pleasant conversation and there was still some anger on their part. I'm sure they have a lot of questions about why I was an absentee father for so long. However, we have had several other conversations since then that weren't so bad. Anyway, I'm picking them up tonight at the Portland airport and they're going to stay with me for a few days. I don't have any unreal expectations that they'll crown me 'Father of the Year' or anything like that, but at least it's a start."

"Well, you have plenty of room in the ranchette for them. What are you going to do with them while they're here? Any ideas?"

"No, absolutely none. I mean, what do you do with your two sons when you haven't seen them in over three years? I've been trying to think of things they might enjoy." He ran his hand through his hair, clearly agitated.

"I kind of remember you said they were teenagers when you left

California. How old are they now?"

"Kevin's eighteen. He's a freshman at Chapman College in Southern California. Josh is sixteen and he's a junior in high school."

Kelly turned around in her seat and motioned for Madison, who had just returned from her cosmetology classes, to come over to the booth. "Madison, we have a little question for you. Doc's two sons are coming to Oregon tonight for a visit. One's your age and the other one's two years younger. Got any ideas on what Doc can do to entertain them?"

She stood there for a moment, lost in thought. "Yeah, why don't you plan on them shore fishing with my dad. He still has pretty good luck catching fish out of the bay and that might be a fun thing for them to do. The other thing that might interest them involves Brandon. Over the past few months, we've become pretty good friends. Anyway, he's on semester break this week and he's just the age of your oldest son. As you know, he's a freshman at Oregon State University. He and I were planning on going horseback riding this week, but I'm sure he wouldn't mind if they came with us. We could also take them down to the tide pools below his ranch house and they could look for some jade on the beach. That should keep them busy for a while."

"Madison, thanks. Those are great ideas," Doc said. "Would you ask your dad about the fishing? I have a fear of boats, so I'm not taking them out in the bay, but I'd love to go fishing with your dad and them as long as we fish from the shore. I know Brandon and I'll give him a call this afternoon. Again, thanks for the suggestions."

"Doc," Kelly said, "I've lingered long enough. Don't worry. I'm sure it will work out and I'm so glad for you."

"I'm happy, but at the same time I'm scared. This is kind of a big deal," he said with a worried look on his face.

"Look at it this way. They're the ones taking a real leap of faith. They must have some feelings for you or they wouldn't have agreed to come visit you," she said as she headed back to the kitchen.

*****

"Jim, do you remember when you told me about going out to the White Cloud Retreat Center and how you thought that Zen Master, Scott Monroe, was doing the Devil's work? Well, look at this. It says in the paper that someone killed him. Someone else probably agreed with you and took care of him. Good thing. Now maybe they'll close that evil place." When she walked out of the room, she missed the smirk on Jim's face.

CHAPTER TEN

"I'll see all of you tomorrow. Enjoy your evening," Kelly said a couple of hours later when Roxie, Madison, and Charlie prepared to leave for the day. "Better stay home, if you can. One of the customers told me they heard on the news that a big storm's expected tonight."

Within minutes after they left, the door opened and Mike and Rebel walked in. Rebel headed to his old bed, clearly not happy that Lady was already in it. He tried to nose her out of it, but the growing puppy stayed where she was, claiming her spot. "Good afternoon, Love. Coffee still hot?" Mike asked.

"Sure is. I just turned it off and was getting ready to make a batch for tomorrow's early birds. Sit down. I'll be back in a second with it." Moments later she set a steaming cup of coffee in front of him along with some cream and sugar. "There you go. Have you eaten lunch?"

"No. I've been on the phone most of the morning. If you've got something, I'd love it."

"How about some manicotti? I was going to bring the last of it home, but if you like, you can have it here instead."

"Is that the Italian dish that has big noodles stuffed with chicken? The one you make with a lot of marinara sauce and cheese?"

"Yep. I know it's one of your favorites, so I figure if it it's good enough for you, it's probably good enough for everyone else."

"So is that what I've become? The official taster for Kelley's Koffee Shop? Try it out on Mike first and see if it's a go? It's sort of like what was done in medieval times. The king had an official taster who tasted all of his food before he ate it to make sure there wasn't any poison in it. Things don't really change with time, do they?"

"Yeah, you're probably right, but I'm not so sure you ever met a food you didn't like. No, I take that back. I remember you telling me that even the smell of brussel sprouts makes you sick. If you've noticed, I've never tested that theory. I'll go reheat the manicotti for you. Cold pizza is good. Cold manicotti not so much."

A few minutes later, he pushed his plate back and sighed. "Kelly, I wish you'd make that more often. It really is one of my favorites."

"I'll keep that in mind. Now tell me about your day. Did you find anything out about Luke and Scott's past?"

"Yes, I did, but first I need to tell you about a weird feeling I've had almost all day. I feel like somebody's watching me. I'm probably just spooked because of Scott's death and imagining it. Anyway, let me get back to your question. They're from a small town in Eastern Washington. Scott must have been charismatic from the day he was born. I spoke with a high school secretary who was just about to retire and she told me she remembers when he was a student at the high school. He was the student body president and homecoming king. She said he was very intelligent and everyone predicted he'd make something of his life, but nobody knew just what it might be. He was even voted 'Most Likely to Succeed.' When she heard he'd achieved almost an idol-like status in some eastern spiritual circles, she told me she was shocked because he'd been a real ladies man, even at that young age."

"Well, I don't know much about Zen Buddhism, but I don't think you have to be celibate to be a Zen Master, although I think he'd mentioned that he was. Maybe I'm wrong."

"I don't think you are, Kelly. His website and a number of articles I read about him mentioned that he was celibate and a vegetarian. Evidently he didn't believe in eating meat because he'd taken a vow not to take the life of anything living. Something else I learned was that alcohol use is not prohibited by the Zen Buddhists, just excessive drinking and becoming intoxicated."

"I always kind of wondered how a Zen Master could drink wine and own a vineyard. Guess that wasn't an issue. Any idea when he became interested in Zen Buddhism?"

"Yes, I think so. He majored in comparative religions in college and from what I found out through the Internet, he started meditating about the time he graduated. He went to Japan and studied with several Zen Masters, one of whom gave him a 'transmission,' whatever that is, and told Scott he was ready to teach and no longer needed to have his own teacher. Sounded kind of like a lot of mumbo-jumbo to me. Anyway, he was a guest teacher at a number of different spiritual workshops and seminars and eventually gained enough of a following to open his own retreat center here in Cedar Bay which we know as White Cloud Retreat Center."

"Sounds like he was destined to do this. The one thing I'm curious about is where he got the money to buy the property. Every time I'm there I have to stop and take a moment to look at the breathtaking view from the Center's location. Plus the Center's vineyard covers a lot of acres. It must have cost a fortune to buy it."

"I was getting to that. Evidently their parents were very wealthy. About a year before Scott bought the property and moved here, his parents died in an automobile accident. I spoke with the attorney who handled the estate and he told me Luke and Scott had a violent argument in his office when the wills were read. Luke was furious that Scott was to receive half of the estate outright because Scott wasn't a businessman and Luke felt he'd squander his inheritance on some fly-by-night spiritual thing. He thought Scott's half should have been held in trust for him. That way he would get a modest portion of it every year instead of one large lump sum payment.

"From what the lawyer told me, they had a shouting match right there in his office and he had to step between them to prevent them from getting physical. Luke left his office, furious, and told Scott he never wanted to see him again. The lawyer told me Scott was just as mad. I asked the lawyer if he could tell me how much money Scott and Luke had inherited. He told me it was approximately ten million dollars for each of them."

"Wow, that's a huge amount of money! No wonder Scott was able to buy the Center. I understand Luke worked in the securities business and lived in New York until he suffered a burnout from stress."

"That's partially true, but there's a little more to it than that. From what the attorney told me, Luke squandered away his inheritance by getting involved with a lot of marginal companies that went bankrupt or had owners who embezzled the company's funds. His work history isn't too great either. There was a scandal when one of his clients accused Luke of embezzling some of his assets, but it never could be proven. Nevertheless, the brokerage company he was with let him go and he left under a cloud of suspicion. That was almost a year ago, about the time he came to live with Scott at the Center. They must have had some type of reconciliation, although I couldn't verify what happened between the two of them."

"Well, I'm glad. I always liked Scott so much and I like his brother, too. I remember Scott was so happy when Luke agreed to come to Oregon and run the business side of the Center so Scott would be free to pursue the spiritual aspect of his life. He told me he didn't enjoy the business part of the Center which had become, in many ways, a large money-making machine," Kelly said.

"One of the other things I found out was that the Center was the recipient of a large number of donations. One man who attended one of Scott's retreats and studied with him for a long time afterwards was so taken with Scott that he donated two million dollars to the Center. That was just a few months ago. I haven't been able to look into the records of the Center, but given the nature of Luke's suspicious past and two million dollars of new cash flowing into the

Center, it's on my list of things to do. If someone had a problem handling money in the past, and had previously been accused of embezzlement, they might have a real problem with that kind of a temptation."

"Mike, you can't be serious. Luke? I don't think so. When I saw him yesterday, he was devastated."

"He was the same way when I talked to him right after Scott's death, but keep in mind the old crime solving adage. That's the one that says the majority of people who commit a murder are often very close to the victim, frequently a spouse or a relative. In this case, Scott didn't have a spouse, but he had a brother."

"I refuse to believe it could be Luke. From what I saw, they seemed to be very close."

"Appearances are often deceiving, Kelly. I'd like to think Luke didn't do it, but at this point I can't rule anyone out. I wish I had some solid motives and solid suspects. So far Luke seems to be the only one who could be a suspect."

"Sorry, can't agree with you on that." She stood up and took his plate and coffee cup off of the table. "To change the subject. With all the talk of the Center and their wine and a rainy night coming, I'm going to stop by The Crush on the way home and pick up a bottle of White Cloud Pinot Noir. We can drink it when the storm hits tonight. What do you think?"

"Sounds great. I need to go to the office for a couple of hours and then I'll be home. Rebel, come." Kelly was busy writing out the menu on the chalkboard for the next day and pretended she didn't see Mike slip Rebel a treat from his pocket. Mike stood up and took his signature white Stetson hat from the coat rack and gave her a mock salute as he opened the door with Rebel expectantly following him.

She shook her head. *I can't believe he'd think for a minute that Luke did it. Doesn't make any sense at all. Maybe I can find out something from Jesse down at The Crush that will make Mike look in some other direction.*

*****

He took out the ledger that he kept hidden behind the files in the bottom drawer of his desk. Probably ought to put this in a safer place. That sheriff was asking a lot of questions when he called today. If he decides to get a search warrant, I could be in trouble. The good thing is that Scott's dead. I think he was becoming suspicious. Glad I was able to take that call from the bank manager about him having the checks that Scott had requested. If Scott had taken the call, who knows what might have happened. Yeah, sometimes you just have to take fate in your own hands. Once I get rid of that pesky sheriff and his hash-slinging girlfriend, I'll be just fine. A few more weeks here and off to Mexico I go. Little tequila, warm little Mexican girl, and no rain. I'm just about there. Even if someone discovered that money was missing from the Center's bank account, don't think Mexico abides much by that extradition treaty they signed with the good old U.S. of A. Just as well. A person can get real lost in Mexico when they have enough money. So long, little brother.

CHAPTER ELEVEN

"Come on Lady, time to go. One stop and then we're home to snuggle in for a rainy night." Lady got up from her bed, wagged her tail, and pranced to the door. *I swear that dog understands everything I say!*

A few minutes later she pulled into the parking lot at the rear of The Crush. Kelly had always loved the simplicity of the name and thought it reflected the man who owned the shop. Jesse was unpretentious and so was his shop. There was an old wooden bar where twelve bottles of wine were always available for tasting. Several wooden chairs and tables also provided a comfortable place for customers to sit while they sampled some of the wines that were being featured that day. Although The Crush had wines from all over the world, the main focus was on the wines of Oregon, particularly the pinot noirs. Photos of the annual fall wine crush were prominently displayed on the walls, several dating back to the prior century. This part of Oregon had been growing grapes for a long time and was just now becoming known for the excellent quality of its pinot noir wines.

"Hi, Jesse. How goes the wine business?" she said to the tall man with his grey hair pulled back in a ponytail and a diamond stud in his left ear lobe. She noticed he was dressed in his customary jeans and blue denim shirt. "Sorry I didn't have a chance to talk to you when you were in the coffee shop last week, but I trust Roxie took good care of you."

"Absolutely. She always knows what I want to eat before I know what I want. What can I do for you today?"

"I'd like a bottle of the White Cloud Pinot Noir. Scott Monroe gave me a bottle a few months back and it was delicious. I understand a big storm is coming, so I thought Mike and I might hunker down for the night and enjoy a good bottle of wine."

"Perfect choice for this kind of weather. I heard about Scott's murder and I'm sure sorry. He often came in here and we'd talk about wine. Scott was a lot more knowledgeable about his wine than some of the other vintners who grow pinot noir grapes. Matter of fact, I'm sure a couple of them are hoping his death might put a stop to the Center's ability to produce the top selling pinot noir in the region. It's one of the most popular wines here in the shop and from what Scott told me, all over Oregon."

"I'm surprised to hear that there were bad feelings among the wine growers as it relates to Scott. I don't know much about the wine industry, but I always had the feeling the vineyard owners were kind of like a brotherhood that all shared information and helped one another."

"Most of them do. I only know of two who don't and they're brothers. Their vineyard is next to the Center on the south side of the county road. They've got about thirty acres planted with vines. I've never liked them. They've been in here a number of times and said things about Scott, the Center, and the wines produced there that were not very complimentary. Matter of fact, they even tried to bribe me once. Offered to pay me quite a bit of money if I would sell their wine instead of his, but I refused. I told them Scott's White Cloud Pinot Noir was a big seller for my shop and their pinot noir couldn't match it. They weren't very happy about that."

"I'm sure they weren't. Jesse, do they produce other kinds of wine besides pinot noir?"

"No, their vineyard is planted exclusively with pinot noir grapes. I hear they do a pretty good business selling to a lot of the discount stores at cheap prices. I was talking to one of their employees who stopped in to see what other pinot noirs I sold and he said they were trying to break into the high end wine market with a new pinot noir. I haven't tried it yet. Matter of fact, I really don't want anything to do with Dante or Luca. I just don't care for them.

"Here's your wine," he said, handing Kelly a light brown wine bag with the word "The Crush" emblazoned in bold black letters on the side. "Enjoy it and tell Mike hi for me. I got the invitation to your wedding and I'm planning on being there and at the reception as well. If you're interested, I'd be happy to bring the wine and provide it at cost. Call it my wedding present to both of you."

"That would be wonderful, Jesse, thank you so much! With everything that's happened, I haven't really had much time to put the final touches on the food and wine. Yes, please, I'll definitely take you up on your kind offer. I think we'll have about one hundred people, although a number of them probably won't drink wine. I'll have some soft drinks as well. I've tried to keep the list down to close friends. You know, in a town this small, you could end up with everyone in the entire town coming and that would be a nightmare."

"Consider it done, Kelly. Glad I can do something for you. My family has never forgotten when you brought Dad his favorite foods when he was getting near the end. It was the only thing he looked forward to."

"I was happy to do it. Your father was a wonderful man and every time I serve a customer at the corner table where he always liked to sit, I think of him."

"Well, he thought just as highly of you, believe me. Enough talking. You better get out of here. The wind's really starting to pick up and the sky is starting to look pretty ominous."

"Thanks, and if I don't see you at lunch one of these days, I'll see you at the wedding."

She got in her van and put the bottle of wine on the floor behind her seat. "Okay, Lady, now it's time to go home. Better let you out before the storm comes. Wet fur is not my favorite thing to deal with! Plus I need to get on the computer and find out what vineyard owners in the region have the first names of Dante and Luca."

CHAPTER TWELVE

"Mike, I am so glad to be home. The skies look like they're about ready to open up. I decided we need a fire and like I told you I was going to do earlier, I stopped by The Crush and bought a bottle of White Cloud Pinot Noir. It sounded perfect for a rainy night." Rebel walked over to where she and Lady were standing and looked up at her, hoping for an ear scratch. Kelly bent down and obliged.

"Give me about an hour and then I'll be more than ready for a glass of it. I need to finish up some thoughts on what I have to do tomorrow on the Monroe case. I don't have a handle on it and with every hour that goes by, statistically it gets harder to find the killer. Maybe if I write some things down, I'll get a little clarity. I sure don't seem to have any right now."

"Actually, that would work out well. I need to do a little work on my computer, so I'll see you then." She walked into the bedroom she'd made into her office. It was cozy and inviting with the large couch piled up with pillows she'd needlepointed over the years, the white walls filled with paintings by local artists, and the vase of fresh flowers she always kept on her old-fashioned desk. Books overflowed out of the corner bookcase and she once again made a promise to herself to go through them and donate some of them to the library.

Kelly booted up her computer and Googled "Pinot noir growers Cedar..." Before she could even type in the word "Bay," three vineyards popped up on the screen as well as the names of the owners of the vineyards. It only took a moment to learn that Dante and Luca Pellino were the owners of the Pellino Brothers Vineyard, specializing in pinot noir wines. She scrolled down their web site and read for a few minutes. Just as Jesse had told her earlier, their vineyard wasn't far from Cedar Bay and was located adjacent to the White Cloud Retreat Center, separated by a county road. Luca was the president of the Oregon Wine Growers Association and had recently made a presentation at the annual conference. One article stated that they were well known for doing a high volume of business with discount chain stores.

I think I need to go over there tomorrow after work. Both jealousy and cutthroat business competition could possibly provide a powerful motive for murder. Maybe I'll get a sense of whether or not one or both of them could be the killer. And if nothing else, I can always pick up another bottle of wine. Now off to a glass of wine and dinner. Along with the manicotti that Mike ate the last of, we served baked burritos at the coffee shop for lunch, and they were a huge hit. I brought the leftover chicken mixture home and I've got the rest of the ingredients for them. I'll make a green salad and I've got time to make Mike's favorite ricotta cake. It's about the easiest thing in the world and he loves it. Might help make up for the vegetarian casserole I served him last night.

Two hours later Mike finished his piece of cake and looked over at Kelly. "Sweetheart, I don't know how you manage to do it, but it seems like every meal is better than the last one. You know how I love Mexican food and those burritos were as good as any I've ever had. And the cake! If I dropped dead right here at the dinner table, I'd die a happy man because of that cake."

"Well, if you did, I wouldn't be very happy about it. That would give a whole new meaning to the term, being left at the altar. It would be more like he never showed up at the altar because he overdosed on food two and a half weeks before the wedding. Don't think that would help my coffee shop business."

Mike took his buzzing phone from its holster. "This is Sheriff Mike. Can I help you?" He listened to the voice on the other end for a moment. "Of course I don't mind you calling me at home, Doc, and I don't think your question is the least bit strange. I'm going to be wearing a dark suit at the wedding, so the same would probably be appropriate for you. Let me ask Kelly."

"Tell him that would be fine."

"The boss says that would be fine." He listened to Doc and then raised his eyebrows and looked over at Kelly. "No, she didn't tell me that, but I have to say in her defense that we haven't discussed the case this evening. I'll look into it tomorrow. Thanks for telling me. I'll ask her about it now. Talk to you soon."

He put his phone back in its holster and looked at her. "I'm going to give you the benefit of doubt on this one…"

She interrupted, "If Doc was talking to you about the guy Scott mentioned when he went to see Doc, I was going to tell you all about it. Honest. We just haven't had an opportunity to talk about the case tonight."

"Like I said, I'll give you the benefit of doubt. Doc said you could tell me about it. I'd like to hear it."

"Well, Doc came in for lunch and told me he'd heard about Scott's death and was really sorry. He said Scott came to the clinic to see him recently because he'd gotten a cut from a rose bush in his vineyard and it wasn't healing properly. He mentioned to Doc that he was really angry at one of the men who was taking part in the residential training program at the Center. You probably remember from when you interviewed people at the Center that the people who are in the program have to work in the vineyards. That's how they pay their tuition for the program. It's kind of a trade-off thing. Anyway, Scott told Doc that the guy pruned the vines too short and he was worried that the grapes from those vines wouldn't be very good this year."

"I think that's a pretty far stretch. I don't see someone who's doing Zen residential training being mad enough at the Zen Master for correcting him to kill him. I'll look into it, but I have a hard time buying that one. What's wrong? You look like you're squirming."

"Well, there's a little more to it. Scott also told Doc that a couple of the local wine growers would love it if the White Cloud Pinot Noir wasn't so popular. Scott said he'd made enemies with a couple of them because the Center's wine was considered by wine connoisseurs to be much better than theirs."

"That doesn't seem like anything that would make you squirm. What are you leaving out?"

She stood up and took some dishes over to the sink and began speaking rapidly while her back was turned toward Mike. "Well, I just happened to be talking to Jesse at The Crush, you know where I bought the wine we drank tonight, and he told me that there were two brothers who are vintners and they'd tried to bribe him to sell their wine and not Scott's. Here's the thing. Their vineyard is next to Scott's and Scott was an organic vintner. He didn't believe in using any pesticides or herbicides on his vines. Jesse said it's the new trend for a lot of vintners in this area. He said these two brothers used all types of chemicals on their vines and Scott was always worried that the chemicals would drift onto his property and damage his vines."

"Let me get this straight. You just happened to be talking to Jesse. Strange, you haven't been to The Crush for a long time from what I can remember. No wonder you were squirming. You went there to find out who the wine growers were after you talked to Doc, didn't you?"

She turned around and faced him raising her hands as if in mock surrender. "I don't think it was a conscious act on my part. Honest. Rain was coming and pinot noir sounded like it would be a good idea on a rainy night, and Jesse was talking about how sorry he was that Scott died. One thing just led to another."

"Uh-huh, I'll bet. Okay, I'll bite. Did you find out the names of the vintners?"

"Not from Jesse. When I got home a couple of hours ago I told you I needed to spend some time on my computer and while I was checking my email and doing some bookkeeping, I decided to see if I could find out anything about them, so I Googled them. Jesse had mentioned their first names and I just typed those in along with Cedar Bay pinot noir vineyards and guess what?"

"You found out who the vintners are. Would I be right?"

"Bingo. You win. Their last name is Pellino and they own the Pellino Brothers Vineyard. I knew there was a vineyard on the property next to the Center, but I never thought much about it. Evidently they sell so-so pinot noir wine to several large discount chains and now they're making plans to introduce a new premium pinot noir, hoping to break into the high-end market. I was going to tell you all of this after dinner. I just didn't have a chance. Now you know what I know."

"I think I've met them. Seems to me they were having problems a few years ago with an employee threatening them because they'd fired him. As I remember, they definitely weren't charmers. In fact, they were arrogant and gave the impression they were better than anyone else. Seemed like the kind of men who would enjoy kicking a dog. I better pay them a visit."

"See, aren't you glad I took a few moments and looked them up? I probably saved you some time."

"Kelly, have I ever told you that you see the world tilted at a little different angle than other people do? It's not particularly a bad thing, but at times it drives me nuts."

"I love you too, Sweetheart. Now that the subject of the murder is out of the way, let's enjoy the fire."

*****

Luca, I'd like to propose a toast to our new venture, the Pellino Brothers Vineyard Premium Pinot Noir. With Scott Monroe dead, our pinot noir will soon become the benchmark for the highest quality pinot noir in this area and hopefully, in all of Oregon. Glad we called Mr. Rossi and Guido came out here to Oregon. Pretty smart of him to enroll in those yoga classes Scott taught. Gave him a good opportunity to get close to him. Rest in Peace, Zen Master, Dante said.

CHAPTER THIRTEEN

The next morning, Mike was sitting at his desk at the Sheriff's Office when his intercom buzzed.

"Yes, what is it, Angie?" he asked his long time secretary.

"Sorry to bother you, Mike, but there's a guy on line two from the Oregon Department of Agriculture. He says he wants to talk to you personally rather than to one of the deputies. His name is Bob Waters."

"Okay, thanks Angie, I'll take it." He picked up his phone. "Hello, this is Sheriff Mike Reynolds."

"Sheriff, my name is Bob Waters and I work for the Oregon Department of Agriculture in Salem. I'm the Director of the Toxic Substances Division and Chief Enforcement Officer for the State of Oregon when it comes to prosecuting farmers who use illegal or banned chemical substances in connection with their farming practices. I think we met a few years back when you attended a seminar we sponsored dealing with illegally dumping toxic materials."

"Of course, Bob. I remember you. We were having a problem here in Beaver County with some illegal dumping over at a copper mine on the far side of the county. You gave me some good tips on how to enforce the laws that were on the books. It's nice to hear from you. What can I do for you?"

"Well, I read in the paper about the death of Scott Monroe, the owner of the White Cloud Winery. I was shocked to learn that he was murdered. He was a leader here in Oregon in the growing practice of organic farming, particularly as it relates to vineyards. His vineyard was one hundred percent organic. He refused to allow any type of herbicide, pesticide, or artificial fertilizer to be used in his vineyard. In fact, two years ago we featured his vineyard in our monthly newsletter that deals with the advantages of organic farming. He's really going to be missed.

"Anyway, the reason I'm calling is I wanted to tell you about an incident that happened out at the White Cloud Vineyard a couple of weeks before Scott was killed. He called me and told me he was having a problem with brown leaf spot on some of his vines. He asked me to come out and take a look at a certain area of his vineyard because he suspected the vines in that area had been exposed to some type of toxic substance. A couple of days later I went out to the White Cloud Vineyard, met with Scott, and inspected the vines in question. I told Scott that, in my professional opinion, I thought they'd been exposed to some type of toxic chemical, probably Dead Bang. I also remember telling him I thought it had probably drifted onto some of the vines in his vineyard from an adjoining property. Dead Bang is a powerful herbicide that's used to control the growth of weeds, but it's been banned for years. Unfortunately, some unscrupulous farmers are able to get access to it and use it in spite of the ban. It's a lot cheaper than the legal weed abatement products that are on the market, so that's why they buy and use it.

"Scott's damaged vines were located right next to a county gravel road that leads off towards the Cascades. On the other side of the gravel road is a vineyard owned by the Pellino brothers called the Pellino Brothers Vineyard. The prevailing winds from the Pellino's property blow directly across the road towards Scott's vineyard. It looked to me like the only explanation for the damage to Scott's vines was that some illegal chemicals drifted across the road from the Pellino Brothers Vineyard and damaged Scott's vines. The drifting of chemical sprays in agricultural areas is a big problem throughout the country and numerous articles and seminars have been held instructing farmers on the safe practices that need to be followed in order to avoid it. Obviously, when the Pellino brothers sprayed the illegal toxic chemical spray on the weeds on their property they didn't follow the recommended safe procedures for the application of chemical sprays. If they had, the chemicals never would have drifted onto Scott's property.

"When I told Scott what I thought had happened he became very angry. I've known Scott for a long time and it certainly wasn't normal for him to become so angry. As I'm sure you know, he was a quiet and peaceful man who lived his Buddhist principles on a day-to-day basis. Becoming as angry as he was when I was there was something he normally never would allow himself to do.

"He told me he was going to pay a visit to the Pellino brothers as soon as I left. If he confirmed that they were using banned chemical substances to control the weeds in their vineyard, he said he'd call me and ask me to investigate and take the necessary enforcement steps. I never heard back from him and sort of forgot the whole incident until I read about Scott's death in the newspaper.

"By the way, the state has had several ongoing enforcement problems with the Pellino brothers and their vineyard. They were issued a citation two years ago for using a chemical pesticide that had been banned from use. They didn't fight the citation, paid a $4,000 fine, and agreed not to use that particular chemical in the future.

"Then there was a problem they had with the Oregon Department of Fish and Game. Almost all the vineyards in Oregon have to be enclosed with a ten foot high fence to keep deer from getting into the vineyard and eating the vines. It's illegal to shoot a deer, even when it's discovered damaging a farmer's vineyard. Not long ago, Fish and Game received an anonymous tip that the Pellino brothers were illegally shooting deer on their property and dumping the carcasses in a ravine three miles from their vineyard. A warden found the ravine in question and discovered the remains of twenty-two dead deer in it. He staked out the ravine and watched for the Pellino brothers to see if he could catch them in the act of disposing of an illegally killed deer, but he never could and he had to close the case as unsolved.

"I thought what I've just told you might be of interest to you in your investigation concerning the murder of Scott Monroe. These Pellino brothers are bad apples and it wouldn't surprise me one bit if they were somehow involved in Scott's death. Hope what I've told you helps and if you need anything else from me feel free to call. "

"Thanks, Bob. What you've told me is very interesting and you can take it to the bank that I'll be talking to the Pellino brothers real soon. Thanks again and if you're ever in this neck of the woods, stop by and I'll buy you a cup of coffee."

Well, well what do you know? Sounds like Scott was really angry at the Pellino brothers and apparently was threatening to report them to the authorities for using illegal chemicals on their property. Wonder if he actually went to their place and talked with them? If he did, that might very well be a motive for them to want to shut Scott up for good.

CHAPTER FOURTEEN - DEIDRE

"Roxie, I need to get those mini ham and egg muffins prepared and in the oven. The Bible study group will be here in about forty-five minutes and they requested that I make that particular recipe for them. They told me it's their favorite. That's the least I can do when they come here every week. Keep the large table by the window open. That's where they like to sit."

"Will do. By the way, just an FYI. You know I take a photography class on Thursday nights."

"Yes, I remember you telling me about it. I love the photos you've given me of the plants and flowers that are native to this area and the ocean shots. They're beautiful. I know you made them into postcards for me, but I've actually framed a couple instead and have them in my office at home."

"What a compliment! What I was going to tell you is there's a woman in my class who's pretty weird, but I have to say she's a real beauty. Her name is Deidre Nelson. I've never seen a natural hair color like hers. It's the most beautiful shade of deep red and she has just a smattering of freckles. Anyway, she spends most of her free time out at the Center and at every class she always talked about Scott and how wonderful he was and how spiritual he was and even how attractive he was. Actually, she looks young enough to have been his daughter, but what I wanted to tell you is that she's here at the coffee shop right now. Looks like she's been crying for days. That beautiful face doesn't look so beautiful now, she's so red and splotchy. I know you're interested in what's going on out at the Center, so I thought you might want to know."

"Thanks, Roxie. If she was that attached to Scott I don't think it's unusual at all that she'd be grieving and by the way, you never said why you think she's weird."

"Before she became so involved in the Center, she was thinking of becoming a professional photographer. Last I heard she's still debating whether to do that or go live at the Center and get involved in their residential program, but what threw me one day was when she told me she spent hours photographing her feet. I think that's pretty weird, although the last few months she hasn't mentioned anything about her feet, she just talked about Scott. And the way she talked about him wasn't in a very spiritual manner, if you get the drift of what I'm saying. Let's face it, Scott was an attractive man and she was well aware of it. From what she said, I guess she thought Scott had a crush on her."

"Well, that's interesting, but I think she misread Scott and I think you've gotten the wrong impression as well. Scott claimed he was celibate and from everything I know about him, he held to that."

"Just sayin', Kelly, just sayin'. Just because someone says they're doin' or not doin' something doesn't necessarily make it so."

Roxie's got to be wrong and that young woman was probably misinterpreting Scott's interest in her, Kelly thought as she prepared the savory muffins. *I'll put them in the oven when the church group arrives. I've got a little time before they get here. Think I'll go out and talk to that young woman.*

She walked out of the kitchen and couldn't miss the young woman with the mass of red hair seated in the corner who was dressed in a green sweater, black leggings, and black boots. A dark green wool coat that matched her eyes was lying in the booth beside her.

She walked over to the young woman and said, "Hi, I'm Kelly, the owner. I don't think I've seen you in here before and I wanted to personally welcome you."

"Thanks. My name's Deidre Nelson. I heard you were the one who discovered Zen Master Scott after he was murdered. Is that true?"

"Yes. Mind if I sit down? I take it you know him. Did you study with him?"

"Sure, have a seat. Yes, I've been taking classes from him since he opened the Center. I don't know what..." She started sobbing, trying to wipe the tears from her cheeks. Kelly went behind the counter and got a box of tissues for her. "I'm sorry. I just don't know what I'm going to do without him."

"It's very hard when we lose a beloved teacher. I remember years ago when a priest in our church passed away. The congregants were devastated."

Deidre shook her head from side to side. "You don't understand. Scott was so much more to me than a teacher."

"What do you mean?"

"Nothing. Nothing. I'm just going to miss my teacher. No one can take his place."

"I'm sure it feels like that now, but in time, another teacher will take his place. It sounds so trite, but time does heal things. My husband died when he was very young and I was left alone to raise two small children. At the time, I didn't want to live. Funny, but this coffee shop saved me and gave me a reason to get up in the morning. And believe me, with time it got easier."

"I'm having a very hard time realizing he really is dead. In a minute, my world changed. I had to work later than usual that day and didn't get to the yoga class on time. Actually, I was very late, but I wanted to do the walking meditation that Scott had mentioned the week before. I got to the Center just as the class was walking into the forest. I'd done walking meditations before, so I followed them. I often lose track of time, space, and events when I'm meditating, so I set a buzzer on my watch to go off in fifteen minutes. When it rang I went back to the Center expecting to see Scott and the rest of the class. Several of the others said Scott had been murdered. I ran to the path he always uses when he does a walking meditation and saw him on the ground. The sheriff interviewed all of us and was very kind and friendly to me. I still can't believe it. Maybe it wouldn't have happened if Scott hadn't gone into the forest."

"Well, that's something we'll never know. I was also participating in the walking meditation when he was killed and I remember seeing a woman with red hair pass by me. It must have been you. I'd like to stay and talk to you, but a group just came in that made a special order request and I need to make sure it gets in the oven."

"Thanks, Kelly. I have to get back to work anyway. I work at the photography shop here in town and help Phil with developing customer's photos and all that stuff. Oh, one other thing," she said, looking down as she picked up her coat. "Someone told me you and the sheriff were engaged. Is that true?"

"Yes. We're getting married in a couple of weeks. Why do you ask?"

"No reason. Just curious. He's a very handsome older man and you're quite lucky to have him. Well, anyway, congratulations." She stood up, stuffing a couple of the tissues in the pocket of her coat. She walked over to the cash register to pay for lunch and left.

A few minutes later Roxie said, "Kelly, Deidre left her wallet on the counter next to the cash register after she paid for lunch. What do you want me to do with it? I'd return it to her, but I won't see her until Thursday and she may need it before then. Plus, she probably won't even be in class Thursday since Scott's service is that afternoon. I suppose I could drop it by her apartment after work. I just looked and her address is in her wallet."

"Where does she live?"

"She's in that apartment building near city hall, the one with the brick front and white shutters."

"I know the one. I'll drop it by later this afternoon when I'm running some errands. I need to stock up at the bakery and the market. It's been so busy today that I've run out of a number of things. Do you know her apartment number?"

"Yes. Here, I'll write it down for you. That way you won't have to rifle through her wallet. I told you she was weird and she may not like you doing that."

"You're absolutely right, thanks. I'll put her wallet in the storeroom for now."

CHAPTER FIFTEEN

"Hello, ladies, it's good to see all of you again. I've made the savory muffins you asked for. They're in the oven and they'll be ready in about five minutes. What else can I get for you today?" Kelly asked the six ladies who had come from their weekly Bible study class at the church a block away, just as they did every Tuesday. She took their orders and went into the kitchen to get the muffins.

"Well, I don't care what you think," she overheard Ellie, a large lady with tightly permed blue-grey curls and wearing a black dress, say as she brought the orders over to their table. "It's a good thing he's dead. We lost a lot of the young people from our church to that smooth-talking non-believer. It may be okay to be a Buddhist in Japan or somewhere over in Asia, but it's not right for our residents here in Cedar Bay. We're Christians and we don't need the likes of him around these parts. Me and a lot of others have hated him for a long time for what he's done to our church."

Kelly purposefully took her time as she served the muffins and main entrees to each of them, listening to the conversation taking place at the table.

"Ellie, I met him and I thought he was a good man. Not everyone believes in what we believe in and who are we to say what's right and what's wrong? He provided a place for people to go who would never come to our church."

"My husband and I know it's wrong. Jim had to go out there one time to fix some problem they were having with their electrical power. He said it was an unholy sight, people sitting in a room with incense burning, and a statue of Buddha placed at the front of the room. He told me it sounded like they were chanting something, but he couldn't understand what they were saying. Jim said it sounded like gibberish in some kind of a strange language. He told me he wished God would take Scott Monroe and if he didn't, someone else should. Looks like Jim's wish came true."

She put her head down, picked up her fork in her plump little hand, and began shoving mashed potatoes and gravy into her mouth. She didn't see two of the other women at the table raise their eyebrows and exchange knowing glances.

"You can't be serious, Ellie. Are you really saying you're glad someone was murdered?" one of the other women asked.

"I sure am. We Christians should make sure that weird religions aren't allowed in our city or anywhere else around these parts. There's only one true religion, Christianity, and anyone who believes anything else shouldn't be allowed to come into our community. I'm glad he was murdered. I'd like to shake the hand of the man or woman who did it and thank them."

Kelly couldn't help herself. "Scott Monroe was a good friend of mine and one of the finest men I've ever known. I know of many people he counseled and helped. No, it's not a Christian center, but that doesn't mean anything. After all, most of the world isn't Christian. He provided an alternate place for people to go who wanted to pursue their own spirituality. I think our community is going to genuinely miss him."

"Well, you're entitled to your opinion, dearie, but mark my words, we true Christians are glad he's gone. Take my husband, Jim, for instance. He's one of the purest men of God I know and he told me after he'd gone out to that Center, he'd like to see Scott Monroe dead sooner rather than later."

"I guess each of us is entitled to our opinion, but let me change the subject. I've got ricotta cake or peanut butter cookies for dessert. May I interest anyone in either of them?"

Mae, who acted as the treasurer of the group, said, "Kelly, why don't you bring us a large plate of the cookies and a piece of cake for each of us?"

That woman and her husband have got to be certifiable nut cases. I can't believe anyone who calls themself a Christian would be happy that someone was murdered. It's unbelievable. I'd hate to think she or her husband was responsible for Scott's death, but differences in religion over time have accounted for an awful lot of wars in the world. Wow. This is something else I better tell Mike.

CHAPTER SIXTEEN

Darn. I haven't been to the bank in two days, Kelly thought. *They don't close until 5:00 today, so I still have time to make a deposit. I remember when that drifter came in here a couple of years ago and robbed me. Don't want that to happen again. Fortunately he didn't get much, but with all the customers we've had in here the last two days, if it happened now it would cause some real financial damage to me.*

She filled out a deposit slip and put it in a cloth bank deposit bag. Five minutes later she opened the door of the First Federal Bank and walked over to the teller, her friend Patti. "Hi, Patti. How was your vacation?" Every time she saw Patti she wanted to tell her that wearing her hair in the Farrah Fawcett long blond curled locks look had gone out of style over twenty years ago. Patti looked like she was in a time warp and not a very attractive time warp. The style may have been popular at one time, but now it looked ridiculous on her.

"Great. Over the kids' school break, I took them to San Francisco, and we toured the town. I'd forgotten how many things there are to do in that city and I think we did them all – Chinatown, cable car rides, the street performers, seafood on the pier. It was really fun, but when I came back I was shocked to hear that Scott Monroe had been murdered. He was one of my favorite people. I took a lot of classes from him, including a meditation class for stress relief. I'll probably think of him every time I sit down to meditate."

"I couldn't agree more. I can't figure out why anyone would kill him. Scott was a genuinely fine man."

"He was in here several times in the last couple of weeks. One time he was making a deposit and a beautiful young redhead woman ran into the bank and rushed over to him. I seem to remember her from some of the classes I took out at the White Cloud Retreat Center. Anyway, he shushed her and told her he'd talk to her later. I remember him saying something like, 'This has got to stop. Please don't follow me or take any more pictures. You can come to my classes, but that's it.' I thought that was kind of strange. I almost had the feeling she'd been waiting for him, you know, kind of like she might be a stalker. I've seen a couple of movies lately about women who stalk men and for some reason, that's the first thought that came to my mind. Something else that occurred to me when I heard about Scott's death was wondering if this woman would find some other man to stalk. I know that sounds far-fetched, but she was really intense. Obviously, she made quite an impression on me."

"I think I know the woman you're talking about," Kelly said. "If it's the one I'm thinking of, she was in the coffee shop today and she was really broken up about Scott's death. Did Scott come in here a lot to do his banking? I would have thought someone at the Center would take care of the business end of things so Scott would have more time to teach and pursue his spiritual interests. I know he wasn't particularly interested in the day-to-day operations of the business."

"It struck me as kind of funny, too. Usually all the banking is done by the business operations director of the Center, John Williams. He's been coming here a couple of times a week ever since the Center opened and still does. No, when Scott was here recently it seemed like it was different. He was concerned about some checks that had been drawn on the Center's bank account by his brother, Luke. When Luke started working at the Center, Scott brought him in one day and put him on the account. It was almost as if Scott thought Luke was paying for things that Scott didn't know anything about. I could be wrong, but that was certainly my impression."

"Interesting. Well, I suppose since Scott didn't like being involved in the business operations of the Center, he probably didn't know everything that was being paid for out of the Center's bank account. Well, I've got a few more errands to do before I can call it a day. Glad your vacation was such a success. See you later, Patti."

Lady jumped in the back seat as soon as she saw Kelly walking up to the minivan. Kelly stopped at the market and then the bakery, both of which were far busier than usual. Because she was running late, she knew Mike would begin to worry about her. She took her phone out of her purse after she'd parked in front of Deidre's apartment building and called him.

"Mike, I know I'm running a little late, but I have one more stop to make and then I'll be home. I should be there within thirty minutes or so. Loves," she said in a voicemail message she left on his phone, thinking that he must be running late as well.

When she finished leaving the message, she took the slip of paper with Deidre's address and apartment number on it as well as her wallet from her purse and walked up the steps of the old brick building across from city hall that had recently been converted into an apartment building. There were three floors in it and Deidre lived on the top floor in unit 305.

Kelly walked down the long hall to her apartment. Even though the door was slightly ajar, she didn't feel comfortable walking in. She knocked on the door. When Deidre didn't answer the knock after a minute or so, she pressed the buzzer located on the wall next to the door and said, "Deidre" in a loud clear voice. A few minutes later when Deidre still hadn't come to the door, Kelly stepped into the living room and stood there in total shock. She looked around in disbelief. Every inch of wall space in the small apartment was covered with pictures of Scott and some were even full life-size blow-ups of him. Strangely, there were also pictures of feet, presumably Deidre's, but some looked like men's feet. She remembered what Roxie had told her about Deidre photographing her feet.

This has to be the weirdest thing I've ever seen. I think Patti was right.

Deidre must have been stalking Scott, but why? And who takes photos of feet and hangs them up on the wall?

She smelled incense and noticed what appeared to be a small improvised altar set up in the corner of the room.

How could I have missed that? I must have been so preoccupied with the photographs I never even saw the altar. Good grief. Deidre must have just stepped out for a moment, because the incense is burning and so are the candles. There must be twenty-five photos of Scott on that altar along with fruit, flowers, and candles. From what I've read about Buddhism, I guess this is an altar to honor his death. How totally and completely strange all of this is.

She took her phone out of her purse and snapped several pictures, knowing Mike would never believe what she had seen in Deidre's apartment unless she showed him some photos. She put the phone back in her purse and rummaged around until she found a business card. She wrote a note to Deidre telling her she'd stopped by to return the wallet that Deidre had left at the coffee shop. As she turned to leave, she looked around the room one more time, still not believing what she was seeing.

Deidre has got to have some kind of a major psychological problem. This is definitely not normal. Scott was old enough to be her father and this obsession with him doesn't look like it's a very healthy obsession. And why pictures of feet? Maybe I can find something out about her on the Internet, although I doubt it would explain her fascination with feet. I better get out of here before she comes back. I really don't want to be in this room alone with her.

She returned to her minivan and locked the doors as soon as she got in. "Lady, time to go home. I need to take a long hot shower. I want to get rid of the smell of incense and the memory of that room. It creeps me out to even think about it."

CHAPTER SEVENTEEN

"Sorry I'm late, Mike. Hope you didn't worry about me. I needed to run some errands and they took longer than I thought." She walked over to where he was sitting in his favorite chair looking out at the ocean and enjoying the last rays of the sun reflecting off of the calm water. "I need to take a shower and I guarantee you're not going to believe what I'm going to tell you. I'll be back in a few minutes."

When she returned, she sat across from him, and took her phone out of her purse. First, she told him about her conversation with Diedre and then she showed him the pictures she'd taken in Diedre's apartment. Next, she told him about the Bible study group and the conversation she'd overheard when they were at the coffee shop having their weekly lunch. She ended by telling him about her conversation with Patti. "Well, so what do you think?"

"What I think is that the case is starting to have some suspects. Certainly Deidre seems like one and so does Ellie's husband, Jim. Sounds like both Diedre and Jim probably had a motive to kill Scott. Not anything a normal person would think of as a motive, but from what you're telling me, neither of those two people seems to be real normal. Plus, if Luke was embezzling funds from the Center, he would have had a motive to kill his brother, too. After all, we know Scott was down at the bank asking questions about the Center's account. Maybe Luke found out about it and started feeling enough heat that it prompted him to take some dramatic action."

"So how was your day? Find out anything new and interesting?" she asked.

He told her about his conversation with Bob Waters from the Department of Agriculture and the problems the state had experienced with the Pellino brothers.

"Well, from what you're telling me it sounds like Scott might have had more of a reason for killing them then the other way around. What did he ever do to them to merit death?"

"Evidently they hated him for producing such a top notch pinot noir. Remember Jesse from down at The Crush told you they'd tried to bribe him to sell their pinot noir in his shop and not Scott's, but he refused, saying that Scott's was much better. From what Jesse said, coupled with what Bob told me in my telephone conversation with him today, it only confirms my initial feeling when I met them – that these are not nice people. Maybe they figured if they killed Scott whoever took over the Center wouldn't be as good a vintner as Scott. That's certainly a motive. I mean, if they can shoot and kill that many deer, they probably would have guns with silencers that could kill a man. I thought it was odd when I interviewed everyone at the Center after Scott's murder, and even though a number of them were in the forest when he was killed, not one of them heard a gunshot, not even you. So I'm thinking that whoever did it must have used a gun with a silencer attached to the barrel."

"Mike, enough about the case. You look really tired. Are you feeling okay?"

"This is going to sound really odd, but like I mentioned before, I've got this feeling I'm being watched. It's the strangest thing. I'll be walking somewhere and I feel like a set of eyes are on me wherever I go. Maybe I'm getting paranoid in my old age, but I've been in this business long enough to sense when something isn't right. Plus, I've been getting a lot of hang-up calls from a blocked number. It's only been for the last few days. I don't know what's going on. Oh, by the way, I forgot to tell you that Rich called the phone company to get a copy of the mysterious phone calls that were made to Scott.

Remember, Luke mentioned to you that someone had been calling Scott and hanging up. Well, they were from a blocked number and the phone company wouldn't release the information without a search warrant. I've been reluctant to ask the court for one until I had some stronger facts on which to base the issuance of a warrant. Right now I don't think I have enough for a warrant to be issued by the court."

"You've been in the law enforcement business for a long time and I know you've created some enemies along the way. Can you think of anyone who was scheduled to get out of prison and might be looking for you?"

"No, no one comes to mind. Yes, I've been responsible for a lot of people going to prison, but I've never had a feeling like this. As I said, maybe it's time for me to retire. I have enough years of service that I could if I wanted to. If I did retire, I was thinking maybe I could help you out at the coffee shop."

"You know you're always welcome. I'm glad you're taking Rebel to work with you. Between your gun and Rebel, I think you'll be fine, but I would ask that you keep me up to date. I'm really concerned."

"I've been debating about whether I should tell you this, but I finally decided I should. I just didn't want to alarm you. With the wedding coming up and Scott's murder, I think your plate is full. I didn't want to add to your problems."

"What are you talking about?"

"I went over to The Crush to see Jesse and find out if he knew anything else besides what he had told you. We talked for awhile and he told me Scott mentioned to him he was having a problem with brown leaf spot on his vines and he was really concerned. He told Jesse he was going to call Bob Waters over at the Oregon Department of Agriculture and have him come out and look at some of his damaged vines. That was all Jesse knew. Here's what I'm getting at. When I left The Crush and walked out to my car, I noticed that something had been written on my windshield, probably with a black marking pen. The words said, 'You're next.' I have no idea what someone meant by that. I consider it a threat, but from whom and why, I have no idea. If someone has been watching me, which I've been suspecting, they would know that I was in The Crush and they had to have written the words on the windshield while I was in there. I'm sure it wasn't a random thing. It would take a real idiot to mistake a car with the words County Sheriff written on it for someone else's car."

"This is a conversation I wish we never had to have," Kelly said. "That really scares me. I've always known your job was dangerous and that at times you'd be in danger, but having someone spying on you and writing threatening notes..." Her voice trailed off as tears welled in her eyes.

"Kelly, come here. We'll be fine." He held her in his arms and stroked her hair. "Trust me. I didn't make it this long in this business by taking chances and with our wedding coming up in a couple of weeks, I'm definitely not going to do anything stupid. Okay?" He put his hand under her chin and tipped her face up to his, kissing her. "Actually, I think dinner can wait awhile. If anyone is watching me, I'd like to give them something special to look at." He reached down, picked her up, and carried her down the hall to the bedroom. Rebel and Lady stayed where they were, their doggie radar on full alert to give their masters a little time and make sure they weren't interrupted.

CHAPTER EIGHTEEN

"Kelly, you've got a phone call."

"Thanks, Roxie, any idea who it is?"

"Nope. He didn't say and I didn't recognize the voice."

"This is Kelly. Can I help you?"

"This is Luke Monroe. When you were out here the other day you mentioned that you had a big shoulder. I'm not going to cry on it, but I would like to talk to you about one of the men who works at the Center and is in the residential training program. His name is Blaine Wright and I think he's been acting rather strangely. I'd like to know what you think about him. It may be nothing and I really didn't want to bother Sheriff Mike about it. After I talk to you, I'd like to know if you think I should get in touch with him."

"Sure Luke, I'd be happy to talk to you. Have I previously met this person? I've taken a few classes and workshops at the Center over the years."

"I think you may have met him when you came out here the other day. He was the one who brought you back to my office that day. By the way, I also called to thank you for the casserole. It was delicious."

"My pleasure. I could be at the Center about 3:00 this afternoon, if that would work for you."

"Yes. I'll adjust my schedule accordingly. See you then."

Well, that's interesting. I wonder what he's found out. Could there be another suspect in the case? Why else would he call me?

A few minutes before 3:00 she got her keys out to lock the coffee shop door. "Come on Lady…"

Before she could get the rest of the sentence out of her mouth, Lady was at the door of the coffee shop waiting for her to open it.

This dog is beginning to spook me. I wonder if dogs can have ESP. If they can, I think I've got one. I swear Lady knows what I'm going to say before I even know.

A few minutes later she pulled into the parking lot of the Center. "Stay, girl, I'll be back in a little while." She opened the door of the Center and immediately sensed a difference. Usually it hummed with people taking classes and enjoying themselves. Today, there was almost a desolate and abandoned feel to the Center.

Blaine walked down the hall towards her. "Hello, Kelly. It's good to see you again. Luke is waiting for you in the office." She followed him and walked into the room while Blaine held the door for her.

"Thanks, Blaine, that will be all for now. Kelly, thanks for coming," Luke said. He walked over to the door and closed it. "Please have a seat and here's your empty casserole dish. It really was good and I appreciate you bringing it to me."

"Glad you enjoyed it. I know you're a vegetarian, but if you can cheat a little, I brought you some bacon chocolate chip cookies. They're a favorite at the coffee shop and my personal addiction."

"I shouldn't admit this, but I'm a sucker for bacon. I'll justify it by pretending I didn't know bacon was in these. Thanks."

"Well, what have you found out?"

"You know my brother was a man who rarely got angry. In fact in the year I've been here, I've only seen him angry twice, both in the last month. You may have noticed that there's a vineyard owned by the Pellino brothers located next to our property. The only thing that separates it is a county road that leads up to the Cascades. They grow pinot noir grapes and Scott suspected some of their methods were hurting our grapes. He was a big believer in organic farming and refused to use any chemicals. He thought it was strange that he'd been having a problem with brown leaf spot and he contacted an inspector with the Oregon Department of Agriculture. The inspector came out and told Scott he thought there was a problem with chemicals that may be drifting from the Pellino Brothers vineyard onto our vines. Scott was furious. He went over to their vineyard when the inspector left to confront them, but they were out of town for a few days.

"I don't know if he ever was able to get in touch with them. This all happened a couple of weeks before he died." He sat back in his chair and said, "Kelly, there's something else that a couple of students from the residential program told me that might be of interest to you. They mentioned that when they were working in the vineyard next to the county road, they noticed a lot of expensive cars going in and out of the Pellino Brothers vineyard. They said that the cars seemed to be driven by dark, swarthy, suspicious looking Italian men. One of the students laughed and said if he was going to cast a movie with Mafia members in it, he'd cast it with the people going in and out of the Pellino Brothers Vineyard."

"I can certainly understand why Scott was so angry. Do you know anything about the brothers?"

"I met them for the first time at an Oregon wine conference I attended a few months ago. One of the brothers is the president of the organization. I can't say I liked either one of them. They were very arrogant and I didn't feel comfortable being around them. Of course, that might have been because I heard that they were saying bad things about our wine. Several people told me they were jealous of the success the White Cloud Pinot Noir has had throughout the state.

"I've heard pretty much the same thing about them," she said. "Evidently they felt you might put them out of business since you're a non-profit business and their business is a run for profit business which supports their families."

"That's interesting," Luke said. "Where did you hear that?"

"I honestly don't remember," she said, mentally crossing her fingers behind her back, "and I'm not sure it's all that important. When you called, you mentioned something about Blaine Wright. He's the young man who escorted me in, isn't he?"

"Yes. I told you earlier that there were two times that Scott had recently gotten angry. The second time involved Blaine. As part of the residential training program in Zen Buddhism, we require that the trainees work in the vineyard or in some other capacity here at the Center. It saves us from having to hire people and pay them to perform routine work here at the Center. We feel it's fair because we provide free room and board while they're living here at the Retreat Center."

"Scott told me about it once and it seemed like a win-win situation for everyone involved."

"I've always thought it worked well. From what I know of the situation involving Blaine and Scott, it centered around Blaine pruning the grape vines too much. Scott was afraid that the grapes from those vines wouldn't be good this year. He was really angry about it. I think what made him even angrier was that he had made Blaine the head of the team that worked in the vineyard. Some of the others work in the kitchen or clean rooms or whatever needs doing. Blaine had grown up on a farm, so Scott felt he wouldn't have to explain everything to him. It worked well for several months, but in the last few weeks Blaine seems to have changed. He was always really easygoing and everyone liked him. Lately we've gotten some complaints that he's been surly and unhelpful in a number of ways."

"I'm surprised. I've only met him twice, but both times he's been extremely courteous and pleasant to me."

"Well, here's what I'm getting at. When people come here for the residential training program, they're required to fill out a number of forms about their past such as schooling, illnesses, etc. We need to know everything we can about them because they live in very close quarters and we try to weed out people who may present problems. Scott was in charge of the residential training program and I never saw the paperwork. When people started complaining about Blaine, I pulled his file out and looked at it. I have to say I was rather shocked by what I found out."

"Such as what?"

"Well, for starters, it indicated Blaine had been committed to the state mental hospital for three years."

"Were there any details concerning his mental condition in the paperwork he submitted?"

"No. I'm getting to that. The paperwork simply said he had spent some time in a mental hospital, but had completely recovered. There was no indication whatever of the nature and extent of his mental illness. Evidently Scott had taken him at his word. I called the state mental institution and after being put on hold a number of times and talking to a lot of different people, I was finally able to speak with his treating physician."

"What did he say? This is really interesting."

"He told me Blaine suffered from schizophrenia, a condition which resulted in him suffering from hallucinations and delusions. While he was in there he was given antipsychotic medications and even underwent some electrical shock therapy. He said Blaine was a classic schizophrenic, but he felt that the medication and therapy had helped him enough that he could be released from the hospital. He told me Blaine had become interested in Zen Buddhism and had become fixated on becoming a Zen Master. Evidently Blaine didn't quite know what to do when it came time for his release, so the doctor recommended that he come here and get involved in the residential training program and he did."

"I'm gathering you think there's some tie between his recent behavior and his stay in the mental hospital, is that right?"

"Yes. I told the doctor about his behavior and his immediate response was that he must have stopped taking his medications. I asked the doctor if that could result in him becoming physically violent. Then I told him what had happened to Scott. He explained to me that it's not uncommon for a schizophrenic person to become so physically violent that they are capable of committing murder."

"Are you saying you think Blaine might have been responsible for Scott's death?"

"I'm not accusing anyone, but certainly he would probably know about Scott being in the forest during a walking meditation and he knew the grounds here as well as anyone. What I can't figure out is what motive he would have for killing Scott."

"Didn't you tell me that he was fixated on becoming a Zen Master?"

"Yes, Zeb even told me that Blaine had asked him several times if he would give him transmission, you know, when a teacher tells a student he doesn't need a teacher anymore."

"I've heard the term, but I'm not very familiar with it."

"Evidently Zeb told Blaine he didn't think he was ready and that Scott, as the Zen Master, was the only one who could do give him the transmission he wanted."

"Maybe Blaine thought that if Scott was dead, he could be the Zen Master," Kelly said.

"Could be. Sounds pretty farfetched to me, but I read up a little on schizophrenia after I talked to the doctor and grandiose delusions are often part of the disease and that could have been his delusion. He's asked me several times if I'm going to take over the Center as the new Zen Master."

"What did you tell him?"

"I told him I hadn't made a decision. So, what do you think, Kelly, should I call Sheriff Mike and tell him what I've told you?"

"You know he's my fiancé. I'll tell him about our conversation at dinner tonight, but let me ask you something. Do you think your personal safety might be at risk because of Blaine? Or for that matter, do you think that anyone else might be in danger?"

"No, I haven't felt that way, but I'll tell you this, I'm keeping my .22 pistol on the nightstand when I'm in bed and in my desk drawer when I'm here in the office."

Kelly stood up. "Be careful, Luke. I'll talk to Mike and I'll see you at the service."

"Thanks for taking the time to come out here. I feel better that you know about this. I never thought my brother had an enemy in the world, but now I've just told you about two. I wonder if there are others."

She turned as she got to the door. "What do you know about a woman named Deidre Nelson?"

"I think she's the redhead who comes here a lot. I don't know much about her other than Scott mentioned one time that she was one of the students who wanted the 'halo effect'."

Kelly interrupted him. "What does that mean? I've never heard that term."

"In yoga or meditation it refers to people who want to get as close as they can to the teacher in hopes that whatever powers the teacher has will rub off on them. Scott said she was always in the first row whenever he taught a class. Why do you ask?"

"No reason. I just met her recently and she told me she'd taken a lot of classes at the Center. She was quite broken up over Scott's death."

"Well, I'm not particularly looking forward to Scott's service for that reason. A lot of people idolized him. I have no idea what to expect. Zeb is planning it, but I'll be conducting it."

"Thanks for taking the time to share this information with me, Luke. I appreciate it and I'm sure Sheriff Mike will too."

CHAPTER NINETEEN

Mike's car wasn't in the driveway when Kelly and Lady returned from the Center. *Well, I've got a little time. Think I'll see what I can find out about Deidre Nelson on the computer.* Lady followed her and lay down next to her in the office.

She pulled Google up on the computer and typed in the name "Deidre Nelson." Within a second, information regarding Deidre popped up on the screen. Kelly clicked back and forth taking notes and looking at the screen. There wasn't much information and it didn't take her very long.

She got up from her chair, went into the kitchen, and opened the refrigerator to see what she could make for dinner that wouldn't take much time. She decided on roast chicken, a warm spinach salad, and fried zucchini squash. She'd just finished smearing the chicken with soft butter and putting it in the oven when the door opened and Rebel bounded over to her, followed by Mike.

"Sorry I'm late, but I had to meet with the coroner on my way home. I would have called, but time got away from me. Anyway, we're home and hungry."

"Well, why don't you take off your gun and change out of your uniform. I'll meet you in the living room and we can relax. I didn't get home too long ago and I just put dinner in the oven. I'll start a fire in the fireplace."

"You've got it. Back in a few minutes." Rebel followed him down the hallway.

Glad you're watching out for him, Rebel. Particularly now that it looks like someone's leaving threatening notes for him, hanging up on him, and possibly following him.

The fire made the room inviting and took the chill out of the winter night. "What did the coroner tell you?" she asked when Mike came back into the room wearing jeans and a flannel shirt.

"It was interesting. We knew Scott died from a gunshot wound to his head. The ballistics expert said it was from a .22 caliber pistol. He also told me something that I thought was sort of strange. He said Scott had been shot in the head, just behind his ear. He mentioned in passing that a lot of Mafia victims were killed that way by a close range shot to the head with the bullet's point of entry located just above and behind the victim's ear. I've never heard of the Mafia operating in this area. Weird, huh?"

"I'm not so sure." She told him about her earlier conversation with Luke.

"Well," Mike said, "the brothers have been suspects in my mind pretty much from the beginning, but now I'm beginning to also wonder about Blaine. He certainly would have had a motive for killing Scott. It looks like he wanted to be the Zen Master in a bad way. Maybe he has delusions that he's ready to lead the Center. This means the case has gone from not having any suspects to having several. Right now I've got the Pellino brothers, Deidre, Blaine, Luke, and that religious guy named Jim. I haven't interviewed Jim yet because I can't think of a valid way for me to broach the subject other than as a conversation you overheard and then I'd have to involve you which I don't want to do.

"I wonder if Luke tried to feed you a red herring. By that I mean if Blaine was a valid suspect in the case, it would take the attention away from Luke. Luke has to know that he's considered to be a suspect. He probably has no idea how much I know about him, but he seems to be pretty smart and that would be a good ploy for him to use, shift attention to Blaine and away from himself. Let's face it, he certainly had a lot to gain if Scott died. Scott's attorney, Lem, called me today and said he was filing Scott's will with the court. Half of his estate goes to Luke and the other half goes to the Center. We know Luke's had problems with money before. Greed is always a powerful motive."

"I know you think he's a credible suspect, but I have a problem seeing him do it. Maybe I'm being stubborn, but I just don't think he's the killer. It takes a special kind of person to kill his own brother."

"Maybe yes, maybe no. All I know is that I'm no closer to finding out who the killer is today than I was yesterday."

"Let's change the subject. Did you have any more poison pen notes or hang-ups today? Or did you sense that someone was following you?"

Mike rubbed his cheek with his hand. "I'm baffled by this whole thing. I'd swear someone is following me, but I sure haven't been able to spot them. When I'm driving, I keep a very close eye on my rear view mirror and haven't seen anything. When I'm walking somewhere, I'm extra alert and on the lookout. Again, nothing. I say nothing, but I've been taking Rebel with me everywhere I go and twice today he growled and his hackles went up. Makes me think this whole thing is not just my imagination. And in answer to your question, yes, there was another note today. This time it was handwritten and stuck in the window on the driver's side of my patrol car."

"Well, what did it say?"

"It was bizarre. It said 'Things aren't always what they seem.' I can't even begin to make sense of that."

"What about hang-ups? Have you had any more of those?"

"Yes," he said tiredly. "More than I'd care to count. I suppose I could get a search warrant and try and find out who's calling, but what am I going to tell the court? That I think someone is following me and calling me? That isn't much to go on. Our local judge is a tough nut and I'm not sure he'd buy it. The only things I have that are solid are a couple of notes."

"I don't know what to tell you. Maybe all of these things are associated with this case. I've kind of thought it was something from the past, but maybe not. What I can't figure out is why anyone involved in this case would do those things. I suppose through a process of elimination we could try and find the answer. Jim, the religious guy, doesn't even know he's a suspect. The Pellino brothers may be aware that they're suspects, but I don't see either one of them following you. They've got a winery to run. Luke and Blaine are both out at the Center, so neither one of them would have the time to drive into town just to leave a threatening note on your car. And Deidre? She's mourning Scott. No, it just doesn't make any sense. Let's forget about it for now. It's almost time for dinner.

"Oh, one more thing. Remember when I told you how strange Deidre's apartment was yesterday? Well, I pulled her name up on the Internet today when I got home and there wasn't much information on the web about her. She works in a photography shop and she's originally from somewhere in Arizona. She majored in photography in college. That's about it."

"Well, the world is full of nut cases. She's probably just another one. I'm starving. I'll set the table while you finish up."

"Deal. Does that mean you'll do the dishes?"

"Don't push your luck, Sweetheart."

CHAPTER TWENTY

Thursday morning Kelly opened the front door of her house and walked outside with Lady. It was 5:30 a.m., just before dawn, and a time when the night sky is at its darkest. Lady growled and began to bark furiously. Out of the corner of her eye Kelly saw someone running away from Mike's patrol car which was parked in the driveway. "Lady, stay. Stay." She put her hand on the dog's shoulder, feeling her raised hackles. She walked over to his car and saw a note stuck under the windshield with the words, "Be very careful. I know where you are." written on it. She lifted the wiper it was under and put the note in her purse.

Mike has enough problems without starting his day seeing this. I'll tell him about it tonight. I saw someone, but I couldn't tell whether it was a man or a woman and there's no doubt in my mind that Lady saw something.

It was another busy morning at the coffee shop. The topic of Scott's death was still the number one item of discussion. Many of the customers expressed frustration that the killer hadn't been caught. When Amber had been murdered the previous June, many of the residents of Cedar Bay had bought guns to protect themselves and their families. Once again the people were afraid. A killer was loose in their town and they felt violated. Cedar Bay had always been a place where there had been very little crime of any kind. Now they were dealing with the third murder in seven months. The tension in the air was palpable.

Kelly walked over to the counter and picked up the ringing phone. "This is Kelly, may I help you?"

"It's Luke. I'm really glad you're the one who answered. I'm sorry to bother you again, but remember when we talked yesterday and I told you about Blaine?"

"Yes, of course. I told Mike about Blaine last night and he's going to check him out today through the FBI database that lists persons of interest."

"Well, I don't think he'll be in there for any past crimes. I don't think he's ever been arrested for anything. I think it's more about his mental condition. Anyway, the reason I called is to tell you he's disappeared."

"What do you mean?"

"Just what I said. The residential trainees are required to attend early morning meditations with Zeb as part of their program, but Blaine wasn't there this morning. After the meditation ended, Zeb came to me and asked if I'd given Blaine permission to skip the meditation this morning. I told him absolutely not. We decided to go to his room and find out why he hadn't attended the meditation session. When we got to his room we discovered it had been cleaned out."

"What do you mean by cleaned out?" Kelly asked.

"I mean he was gone and so was everything belonging to him. We went to the parking lot and found that his car was gone as well. I have no idea what it means, other than it's quite suspicious. I thought you might want to tell Mike. I just called his office, but he was on another call and I didn't have time to wait. As you know, Scott's service is this afternoon and I have a lot of things I have to do to get ready for it. From the calls I've been getting, it looks like a lot of people plan on attending, even people from quite a distance. I'm glad I decided to have it from 4:00 to 6:00. That will give people a chance to get to an airport or drive back to where they came from before it gets too late."

"Luke, did you talk to any of the other residents? Did Blaine say anything to them? What did they think of him?"

"Yes, Zeb and I spoke with all of them and evidently he hadn't said a word to any of them about leaving. Many of them said he'd told them he wanted to be a Zen Master, but none of them felt particularly close to him. A few even said they thought his commitment to Zen wasn't real. They felt he was almost frantic about becoming a Zen Master, but it wasn't genuine." Luke was quiet on the phone for a long moment and then said, "A thought just occurred to me."

"Please, tell me whatever you're thinking."

"Well, after you left yesterday, Blaine came into my office and asked me who you were. I told him you were the sheriff's fiancée and we'd been talking about Scott's murder. Then he asked me if I was going to become the Zen Master here at the White Cloud Retreat Center. I told him I'd been thinking about it and yes, I probably would become the Zen Master for the Center. I told him Scott had given me a transmission, so theoretically I had the necessary credentials to do it. Now I'm wondering two things. First of all, he may have been concerned that Mike was getting close to solving the murder, or that he had become a suspect. Who knows what goes through a schizophrenic's mind? On the other hand, maybe he realized he wasn't going to become the Zen Master here at the Center and there was no real point in his staying. I don't know, but those are about the only explanations I can come up with for his sudden departure."

"I think you might be right with either one or even both. I know you're in a hurry, but thanks for telling me. I'll see you this afternoon."

Well that's interesting. Maybe Blaine was the person I saw this morning by Mike's car. Maybe Luke's right and he was concerned that Mike was getting close to solving the case and determining he was the killer.

CHAPTER TWENTY-ONE

Mike closed the door to his office and sat down at his computer with Rebel at his side. Last night he'd remembered that the FBI had a database that identified people who had been designated as "persons of interest" in criminal cases. He'd decided to see if the database had any information on Dante and Luca Pellino, Luke Monroe, Blaine Wright, or Jim Duncan. Even though he and Kelly had talked about Deidre, he didn't feel she had risen to the level of being considered a suspect. It had almost been a week since Scott had been killed and Mike was getting desperate to find the killer. An hour later he sat back in his chair, thoroughly frustrated. His search had come up with nothing.

Well, since I'm getting absolutely nowhere with those four, might as well plug in the names of everyone we interviewed in connection with his murder. Maybe I'm overlooking something.

Halfway through his search, he got a match for Deidre Nelson. He spent a few moments studying the information and reached for his phone.

*****

Detective Joel Ackerman of the Tucson, Arizona Police Department picked up the ringing telephone on his desk and said, "This is Detective Ackerman. May I help you?"

"Hello, Detective. My name is Mike Reynolds and I'm the county sheriff in Beaver County, Oregon. I'm working on a homicide case up here that occurred in Cedar Bay, Oregon. A woman by the name of Deidre Nelson was one of several we interviewed in connection with this case. I ran her name through the FBI database that identifies all persons in a criminal case designated by the investigating authorities as a person of interest. I came up with a hit that listed your department as well as your name and telephone number as a contact for any follow-up requests for information. I was wondering if you might have some recollection or information about a woman named Deidre Nelson that might help me with my investigation."

"I sure do, Sheriff. Don't mind at all sharing the information we have. I was the detective assigned to the case and I clearly remember the facts and circumstances that were involved in it. It was a missing person case with a strong suspicion that some type of foul play was involved. The missing person was a forty-five year old man by the name of Albert Finley. He lived with his wife and family in a house in a Tucson suburb. There were no suspicious activities or signs of any type of trouble in his background. According to all reports, he was a respectable, upstanding and well-liked member of the community. He was a handsome, rather athletic type of guy who liked to go jogging every morning. One morning about ten years ago, according to his wife, he left the house to go for his regular morning jog and was never seen again. His bloodstained shoes and socks were found on a jogging trail not far from his house. For reasons we don't know or understand, after his shoes and socks were removed he walked away, either voluntarily or under threat of force, from the location where his shoes were found. We followed a trail of his bare footprints for a short distance, but then the trail disappeared. I always thought it was pretty strange he'd wind up being barefoot on a remote jogging trail in early spring. It was still very cold at that time of year.

"As part of the work up on the case, I canvassed the neighborhood and interviewed all the neighbors, asking them if they'd seen anything suspicious prior to Mr. Finley's disappearance. The next door neighbor was a woman by the name of Clara Nelson. She was the mother of Deidre Nelson, who at the time was nineteen and living at home with her mother. Mrs. Nelson told me she didn't know anything that would help me with the case. She suggested I talk to her daughter who was at home and in her bedroom.

"Mrs. Nelson, who appeared to be in poor health and was confined to a wheelchair, told me to just walk down the hallway and knock on her daughter's bedroom door if I wanted to talk to her. I knocked on the door and a young woman's voice said 'Come in.' When I walked into the room I observed Deidre, who was an attractive looking young nineteen year old woman with bright red hair, sitting at a small writing desk in the room. I immediately noticed that there were ten or twenty photographs of the missing man, Albert Finley, tacked up on the walls of her bedroom. Several of them were life-size blown-up photographs of Mr. Finley. After I explained to Deidre the purpose of my visit, I asked her why she had the photographs of Mr. Finley tacked up on the walls of her bedroom.

"She explained that she wanted to become a professional photographer and was studying photography at a local community college. One of her class assignments was for each student to prepare a collection of photos of some person that they knew. It could be a family member, a neighbor, a fellow student, or whoever. She told me she'd selected Mr. Finley, but she decided not to tell him about her project and just take photos of him without his consent. She said she thought using that process would make her photos of him more natural and lifelike, without a lot of posing and phony smiles. All of the photos she took of him were taken with a camera equipped with a telephoto lens. Other than that, Deidre denied knowing anything about Mr. Finley's disappearance.

"I thought her explanation of why she had the photographs of Mr. Finley displayed on the walls in her room was rather suspicious and for that reason I entered her name in the case file as a person of interest. A few days later I contacted the professor at the community college who was teaching the photography class and he verified that Deidre and his other students had each received an assignment from him along the lines that Deidre had described to me. I asked him why he required life-size photographs. He told me that was not part of the assignment and he had no idea why a student would do that unless they wanted to see if they could enlarge the photographs they'd taken. According to him, some of the students hoped to work in a photo lab and that could possibly be the reason.

"We never found Mr. Finley and there were no active leads for us to follow. About two years after he went missing, the case was closed and transferred to our cold case files. When the case was closed and as part of the routine file closing procedure, one of our administrative staff members entered Deidre's name as a person of interest in the FBI database you referred to earlier. By the way, about the time we were getting ready to close the case, I went back out to the neighborhood to have a final interview with the neighbors and see if they had any new thoughts about what might have happened to Mr. Finley. When I was there, I learned that Mrs. Nelson had died the previous year and that according to the neighbors, her daughter, Deidre, had moved to the Pacific Northwest, but none of them knew where. That's about all I've got, Sheriff. Don't know if any of that can help you, but if you need anything else, feel free to call me."

"Thanks, Detective Ackerman. I really appreciate your input. Not sure if it will help, but it just might. Again, thanks," Mike said as he hung up the phone.

Now isn't that interesting. Deidre took numerous photos of Mr. Finley in Arizona, just like she did here in Oregon of Scott Monroe. I wonder if this is a pattern of behavior on her part. It's not uncommon for a young woman to fantasize about an older man. I've heard of some who start stalking a man and taking pictures of him without his knowledge or consent. Stalk, photograph, fantasize, and then kill, is certainly a possible modus operandi of a deranged individual. I wonder if she was stalking Finley when he disappeared. For that matter, I wonder if she was stalking Scott. I've got meetings the rest of the day and then the service for Scott this afternoon, but talking to Deidre has become a high priority for me. I'll do it tomorrow.

CHAPTER TWENTY-TWO

Kelly happened to look up just as the door of the coffee shop opened and Diedre walked in. "Good morning, Deidre. How are you doing today?"

"Much better. I wanted to come by and personally thank you for bringing my wallet to me, so I decided to take an early lunch. Is there any special table I should sit at?"

"No, this is the calm before the storm. Sit wherever you want. I'll be with you in a minute."

Kelly went into the kitchen to check on Charlie and see how he was doing. He'd stepped out the back door and was smoking a cigarette. "Jes' takin' a little break before the lunch crowd gets here, Boss."

"Take your time. We have a lull in the action at the moment."

"Got a message for you from Dad. He says he had a dream that you were in danger. Ya' better take it seriously. Dad's dreams are kinda legendary on the reservation. If he dreams something, you can almost take it to the bank that it's probably gonna happen."

"Did he say what kind of danger I was in?"

"Nope. Only that you better be very careful for the next few days."

"Swell. That's just what I wanted to hear. Okay, tell him I'll be extra careful."

"That's not all, Kelly. He said to tell you that Mike's in more danger than you are."

Kelly felt a chill run along her spine. She considered Charlie's father, Chief Many Trees, to be a friend and knew he was not one to speak lightly. If he said she and Mike were in danger and should be careful, they probably should.

"Charlie, we better get back in there. Tell your dad thanks and we'll be very careful."

"Have you decided what you'd like to eat, Deidre?"

"Yes. I'll have a bowl of chili and a cup of hot tea. It's cold outside and that sounds good."

"I'll be right back with your order."

"Oh, I'm in no hurry. Phil thinks my work is pretty good, so he cuts me some slack if I run a little over for my lunch break. I understand you're going to be marrying the sheriff in a couple of weeks. How did you two meet?"

"The same way I met you. Here at the coffee shop. He'd been coming in here for a long time and one day he said how much he liked my cooking. I invited him to dinner and that was how it all began. He was divorced and I was widowed. He's a fine man and I'm honored that he'd want to marry me. Why do you ask?"

"He interviewed me the other day out at the Center, you know, the day Scott was killed. He was very kind to me. I was crying so hard I had trouble talking and he put his arm around me and consoled me. I thought that was a very nice thing for him to do. He made an impression on me because he knew about my shoes."

"I'm sorry, but I have no idea what you're talking about."

"Well," Deidre said. "I was in the group of students that had assembled near the murder scene right after you discovered Scott's body. Sheriff Mike interviewed each of us and then we were released. I went to my car to change my shoes and I put on some different shoes, actually they were Christian Louboutin sandals. You know, those are the ones with the red soles. After I changed shoes, I decided to go back into the Center to go to the restroom before driving home. As you know, the Center has a policy that no one can wear shoes while they're inside it. After I used the restroom I went back out to the porch to put my sandals on. While I was putting them on the sheriff walked by and asked me if they were Christian Louboutins. I was curious how he knew and he said he'd just read an article about them in the business section of the Portland Tribune. He said he spotted the red soles on my sandals. I was impressed. I've never met a man who knew something like that. You're a lucky woman."

"Yes, I am," Kelly said. "I don't want to make Phil over at the photography shop mad at me for keeping you so long, so let me get you your chili and tea."

Mike knows about Christian Louboutin shoes? That's strange. And even stranger that someone would remember that.

A few minutes later Kelly returned and said, "Here's your order, Deidre. Enjoy! I need to talk to some other customers. See you later."

"You're going to the service for Scott this afternoon, aren't you? I'll see you there."

"Yes, I'll definitely be there," Kelly said.

Kelly locked up the coffee shop as soon as she and her employees finished cleaning it up and getting ready for the next day, anxious to get home and change clothes. Mike was meeting her at home and they were going to drive to the service together.

*****

"Hi, Sweetheart, be with you in a minute. I need to change clothes," Mike said when he opened the front door.

"Actually, Mike, I think you better wear your sheriff's uniform. Luke told me that people usually wear white to solemn occasions like this and I don't think you have a pair of white pants. As you can see, I'm in white, but it's a lot easier for me to be dressed that way than it is for you. Everybody knows you're the sheriff and it might make some of the visiting dignitaries feel good, knowing that the sheriff is there."

"That's a good point. Okay, you sold me. Let me wash my face and hands. Why don't you let the dogs out before we go and I'll be back in a couple of minutes?"

On their way to the Center, Kelly said, "Deidre was in the coffee shop today and told me you'd complimented her on her Christian Louboutin shoes. She said no one else had ever done that. I think you're a hero in her eyes because of it."

"That was the strangest thing. I'd read about them in the paper just the day before and then I saw this pair of sandals with red soles. Talk about coincidental!"

"We're almost at the Center, but I need to tell you what Luke told me today about Blaine." She recounted her earlier conversation with Luke about how Blaine had mysteriously disappeared.

"That certainly is suspicious. You'd think he'd at least wait until after the service to leave. That's really odd. Any idea where he went?"

"No, from what Luke said, he and Zeb talked to all of the other people who were in the residential training program and no one knew anything. Evidently he wasn't well-liked by them. They thought he'd changed recently."

She thought back to the note she'd found early that morning. "Mike, did you find any notes today?"

"No. It seems to have quieted down. I've decided it's just paranoia on my part."

"I wish that was true, but I don't think it is. When I walked out the door this morning to leave for the coffee shop, I saw someone running away from your car. I would have thought I was imagining it, except Lady growled and barked. Her hackles were raised, so I'm pretty sure it wasn't my imagination. Then I went over to your car and there was a note on it that said, 'Be very careful. I know where you are.' Here it is," she said, opening her purse and handing it to him.

"Okay, this is definitely not imagination working overtime for either one of us. Remember that gun I bought you a few months ago? Well, as soon as we get home I want you to put it in your purse and carry it with you all the time. I have mine and just like you asked me to do, I'll make sure to take Rebel with me wherever I go. You do the same with Lady. I know she's young, but from what I've seen, she'd protect you. Deal?" he said as he parked the car in the Center's parking lot.

"Yes, although it's a deal I wish I really didn't have to make. I don't like to think of either one of us being in danger. Oh, there's one more thing," she said, putting her hand on his arm to keep him from opening the car door. "Charlie's father wanted to get a message to us. Charlie told me that Chief Many Trees had a dream about us and he wanted to warn us to be careful, because we're both in danger."

"That's just great. It's not bad enough that I feel like I'm being watched, I'm getting threatening notes, and you're seeing people running away from my car, now Chief Many Trees has some vision or dream that we're both in danger. And the thing is, I've heard that old guy is usually right about his dreams and visions. I'll be so glad when this case is solved. I'm starting to get spooked and that's a pretty new feeling for me."

"Well, we need to put it behind us for now. This is a service for Scott and I want to honor his memory. I know you do to. Let's go in."

CHAPTER TWENTY-THREE

The large meditation room of the Center was completely filled with mourners who stood, looking at the altar and the robed priests who were in front of it. Most of the people wore white with the exception of the priests, including Luke, who were dressed in brown and black robes. Kelly looked around and nodded to several people she knew. A few minutes before 4:00, Deidre entered the room and stood behind Mike and Kelly. Promptly at 4:00, Luke asked the mourners to put their hands together, hold them in front of their hearts, and keep them there for the duration of the service. He told them that each aspect of the service had a special significance. The chanting they would hear was the teaching of the Buddha; the scent of incense purified the participants; and the smoke rising from the incense is said to deliver the thoughts and prayers of the mourners to the decedent. At the conclusion of the one-hour service Luke stepped forward and thanked everyone for coming. He asked them to stay and enjoy the light refreshments which had been placed on tables on the porch.

Kelly and Mike walked out to the porch and helped themselves to the fruit offerings many people had brought as well as tea. Mike looked around to see if any of the people he had put on his list of suspects had attended the service. He knew it was very common for the killer to attend a service or funeral for the decedent. The only people there who were on his list were Deidre and Luke. She wasn't anywhere near the top of his list and she'd been attending classes and workshops at the Center ever since it had opened, so it was to be expected that she would be present. And since Luke was Scott's brother and the managing director of the Center, as well as a Zen priest, he would certainly be expected to be there as well. There was no sign of the Pellino brothers, Blaine Wright, or Jim Duncan, which didn't surprise Mike given his strong aversion to any Eastern religions.

Kelly felt a tap on her shoulder and turned around. It was Jesse, the owner of The Crush. "Hi, Jesse. I don't know much about Zen Buddhism, but that was a lovely service, don't you think? Have you ever taken any classes or workshops from the Center?"

"No. I came because of the relationship Scott and I developed over our mutual interest in wine. I'll be curious to see what happens to the wine produced here. I know he was interested in spiritual matters, but he was also very well versed in all things related to wine. He constantly read up on the latest techniques and what he could do to improve his wine. He was one of those people who had a very refined sense of taste. Scott could tell you if there was a hint of a berry or smoke or whatever with one sip of wine. Actually, I've seen him smell wine while he swirled it in his glass and identify every flavor in it. I've been around wine a long time, and my nose and taste is a lot better than most people's, but he had me beat by a mile."

"I really never knew that side of him. The only thing I know about wine is whether I like it or not and I always seem to like the Center's wine. I wonder what the Pellino brothers will do now that Scott's dead."

"I heard a rumor they were going to try and buy the Center. One of my customers told me that the brothers had some ties back East and they were being financially backed by them. Given the brothers' Italian names and everything, I wonder if we're going to see some Mafia money roll into Cedar Bay."

"Oh, I hope not. We've got enough problems as it is."

"To change the subject. I've ordered the wine for your wedding.

Since it's winter, I ordered more red than white and I also ordered some Pellegrino sparkling water in case people don't drink alcohol or prefer not to drink during the day. Since you're being married at 10:00 a.m. and the wedding celebration is at noon, I'll come to the house directly after the wedding and get set up. I'll have the white wine on ice in the van. I've got napkins and glasses, so you don't need to worry about anything."

"That's wonderful, Jesse. I really appreciate you taking care of it and thanks for giving me a discount on the price!"

"My pleasure. I've got to leave and get back to the shop. Talk to you later."

Kelly turned around and noticed that Mike was talking to Deidre. She walked over to them and heard Mike say, "Since you're off tomorrow, I'll probably be there around two or three. See you then." Deidre walked away and Mike turned to Kelly.

"Are you about ready to leave? I need to go into my office for a few minutes, but I'll take you home first."

When they were in the car, Kelly asked Mike what he and Deidre were talking about. "I told her I needed to talk to her and asked when would be a good time. She told me she was off tomorrow. You heard me tell her I'd be at her apartment in the afternoon."

"She seems to have calmed down since I saw her at the coffee shop the other day. I noticed she had tears in her eyes during the ceremony, but I did too. I guess maybe the passage of a little time is helping her. Oh by the way, I learned something interesting from Jesse. He heard from one of his customers that the Pellino brothers had ties to people back East who wanted to bankroll them so they could buy the Center. Jesse wondered if those were Mafia ties."

"That's interesting. Particularly since the ballistics expert said that the bullet placement that killed Scott was very similar to those seen in Mafia murders. Wonder if the Pellino brothers had a contract out on Scott? Maybe someone came out here to kill him. Wouldn't that be something? The Mafia in sleepy little Cedar Bay. That really would be a case of truth being stranger than fiction."

He stopped the car in the driveway to let her out. "See you in a little while. I shouldn't be too long. Remember, I asked you to get your gun and keep it with you."

"I will, but wait a minute while I get Rebel. I want him to be with you. Deal?"

"Deal!"

CHAPTER TWENTY-FOUR

A number of the people who came to Kelly's Koffee Shop on Friday morning had attended the service for Scott the previous afternoon and wanted to see what everyone else had to say about it. It amazed them how many people had traveled to their sleepy little town from all over the world to attend the service of a man they'd simply known as Scott – a man who dressed in jeans and was a winemaker. Obviously, from the number of international high-ranking spiritual people who had attended the service, there was a lot more to this man than they'd realized.

In keeping with his habit, promptly at noon Doc walked in with Lucky. "Kelly, when you have a minute, I'd like to talk to you," he said, grinning broadly.

"Well, from the smile you're wearing, I'm making an assumption that your sons' visit was a success. I'll be with you as soon as I can. Take a seat."

"Okay," Kelly said, a few moments later. "I've got a little time. I want to hear all about it."

"Kelly, I don't know when I've been so happy. It couldn't have gone any better. Just as Madison told us, Brandon was on a school break and he took the boys horseback riding on his ranch. Madison went too. I wonder if there's something going on between those two.

Anyway, my sons are city boys, so all of this being in the great outdoors and enjoying nature is really new to them. Matter of fact, I don't think they've ever been horseback riding before, and they loved it. When they finished riding, Brandon took them down to the tide pools below his ranch house and showed them how to look for jade. They both found several pieces and can't wait to show them to their friends."

"I'm so glad. I've been thinking about you all week."

"Well, that's not all. They loved Lucky which didn't surprise me. We used to have dogs and a big back yard, but when I left to come here, their mother didn't want to deal with yard work, so they sold the house and moved into a condominium. My ex-wife went to work as a nurse and with the boys in school and no lawn for a dog to play on, they didn't feel it would be fair to the dog to stay cooped up all day, so they made a decision not to have one. The boys have always had a dog and they said not having a dog to come home to and me being gone were pretty rough things for them to adjust to."

"Poor things. Their lives really changed. Dad gone, no dog, and living in a new place."

"Yeah. We talked a lot. I think they understand a little more why I left and moved up here. Anyway, Madison's dad took them shore fishing and they both caught a couple of fish. That was pretty exciting, but the best thing I've saved for last."

"Out with it, Doc. Roxie's looking over here and it probably means my time with you is about up."

"Last night Liz came to dinner and to meet them. She's done a lot of work with teenagers and children whose parents are divorced, so she had a pretty good idea what to expect."

"Doc, I'm curious. How did you introduce Liz to them?"

"I told them I'd asked a woman I worked with at the clinic to come for dinner. I mentioned she was a psychologist, but I didn't tell them I had been seeing her outside the clinic."

"That was probably a good idea."

"Well, here's the best part. Liz, unbeknownst to me, is a gaming freak. You know I don't have a television, but I've got an iPad and iPhone and the boys had theirs as well. I guess Liz always travels with both of hers, so the three of them spent an hour before dinner playing games on their mobile devices while I was cooking dinner."

"I'm curious. What did you fix for dinner? That must have been a tough menu to come up with."

"I remembered that the boys loved a dish their mom used to make for them. It's a slow cooked beef burgundy served over noodles. I made it last Sunday and froze it, so all I had to do was defrost it and cook it for another hour. The noodles are super easy and I've got a recipe where you don't even have to drain them, they cook in butter and water in just a few minutes."

"I'm getting hungry thinking about it. If you don't mind, I'd like to have the recipes for both of those."

"I'll bring them Monday when I come in. I also had asparagus with some garlic, olive oil, and parmesan cheese. Made some biscuits and finished it off with that cheesecake recipe I got from you a couple of months ago."

"Well, I'm impressed and I bet the three of them were too. As I remember, Liz loves to eat, but cooking isn't high on her priority list. Good thing she has you."

"The dinner was great, but what was even better was about an hour after dinner Liz said it was time for her to leave. She told the boys she knew it was our last night together and she didn't want to intrude on our time. They both insisted she stay and the four of us talked about school, their sports, and a million other things. It was one of the best nights of my life. They loved Liz. After she left, they told me they wouldn't come back unless I made sure that Liz was included in everything we did. If they hadn't liked her, I don't know what I would have done."

"Doc, are you thinking of marrying Liz?"

"Funny you should ask. I'm thinking of asking her tonight to be my wife. The boys had an early flight out of Portland and I had a little time after they left, so I went to a jewelry store. I guess I can show you this," he said, pulling a small jewelry box out of his pocket and opening it. "What do you think?"

"It's absolutely beautiful! What woman wouldn't love a diamond like that? But I have a feeling she'd marry you if you only had a wedding band for her. I know tomorrow's the weekend, but I want to hear what she says. Okay?"

"Promise. You'll be the first to know. I keep having to pinch myself to make sure that all of what's happening to me is real. I'm practicing medicine again, my boys are in my life, I've got a great dog, and there's a good chance a wonderful woman is going to say yes when I ask her to marry me. I'm not sure life can get any better than this."

"Doc, I've got to get back to work." She stood up from the table, walked around it to him, and lightly kissed him on the cheek. "I'm so very happy for you. You deserve all of this. Don't forget to call me tomorrow."

CHAPTER TWENTY-FIVE

It had been a long week and Kelly was ready for the weekend. After she locked the door to the coffee shop, she and Lady walked over to where her minivan was parked in the lot adjacent to the pier.

Darn. I just remembered that I need to renew my driver's license over at city hall and time is running out. The next two weeks I'm not going to have time to take care of anything but working and getting ready for the wedding, plus Julia and Cash will be here in a week. I better take care of it now. Hate to waste my time doing things like that, but it would just be my luck to get a speeding ticket and then word would get out that the sheriff's new wife was driving on an expired license.

She pulled into the Cedar Bay City Hall parking lot and noticed what she thought was Mike's patrol car parked across the street. As far as she knew, he was the only one who drove a car with the words "County Sheriff" written in white on it. She could make out Rebel's form in the car and it looked like he was barking. He was standing in his usual place on the passenger seat with the window partially open. When she opened the door on her minivan, she clearly heard him barking. *That's strange,* she thought. *Rebel never barks when he's left alone in the car.* Lady jumped out of the minivan and whimpered. Mike had given Kelly a key to his car in case it was blocking hers in the driveway and she needed to move it early in the morning in order to get to the coffee shop while he was asleep.

She walked over to Mike's car, unlocked the car door, and let Rebel out. His barking turned into a deep growl and the black hackles along his back were raised. He hurried over to a nearby building with white shutters and looked back at Kelly and Lady, as if to say "Follow me."

That's Deidre's apartment building and now I remember that Mike was going to her apartment today to talk to her about what he'd found out from that Arizona detective. What I don't understand is why Rebel's almost in an attack mode.

Lady, Rebel, and Kelly rode the elevator up to the third floor and got out. Rebel sniffed the carpeting as if he was searching for a scent. Kelly and Lady hurriedly followed Rebel down the hall to Deidre's apartment and stopped in front of the closed door. Kelly put her hand down, indicating to the dogs that they were to stay where they were. She heard Deidre's voice inside the apartment. Kelly put her ear to the door and listened.

"If I can't have you, I'll make sure Kelly can't either. I'm going to take your shoes off. I want to get a picture of your feet to remember you by. You'll never know," she heard Deidre saying in a faraway sounding voice.

Kelly didn't hear any sounds or words coming from Mike. Deidre continued, "You're just like Scott. I offered myself to him too, but just like you, he said no and you know what happened to him."

Kelly took her gun out of her purse and looked at both of the dogs. Rebel's hackles were raised and Lady was watching Rebel and trying her best to do what Rebel was doing. Kelly put her finger to her lips and shook her head. The dogs stood as close to her as they could. She could feel Rebel's body quivering.

Where could Mike be? He must be in the apartment. Kelly turned the door knob as quietly as she could and to her surprise, the door was unlocked. She opened it slightly and peered through the slit. She involuntarily put her hand up to her mouth to stifle a scream. Mike was lying on the floor, not moving, while Deidre was in the process of carefully removing his shoes and socks. Kelly raised her eyes and saw several life-like blown-up photographs of Mike tacked on the wall where a few days ago there had been photographs of Scott.

Suddenly, it was crystal clear to Kelly. Deidre had killed Scott and was getting ready to kill Mike. She knew she had to do something and she had to do it fast. Deidre was bent over Mike, totally engrossed in trying to remove his shoes. Kelly swung the door open, yelled "Rebel, Attack," and fired her gun. She aimed to the left of Deidre, intending to scare her. Deidre reached for a gun that was lying next to Mike's foot, but before she could reach it, Rebel jumped on her, pinning her to the floor while Lady grabbed hold of the bottom of Deidre's slacks, preventing her from moving. Kelly ran over to Mike and put her ear on his chest. She could hear him breathing.

Thank God. Deidre must have only knocked him out. "Rebel, Lady, Guard," Kelly said in a loud commanding tone of voice. Both of the dogs stayed exactly where they were, Rebel inches from Deidre's face, and Lady with Deidre's pant leg in her mouth. Both of them were growling. Kelly scooped up the gun lying on the floor and kept her gun on Deidre while she called 911. "Officer down! Sheriff Reynolds is unconscious. I need help immediately! I'm on the third floor of the apartment building across from city hall in apartment 305. Hurry!"

Within minutes she heard footsteps pounding down the hall. Rich, Mike's chief deputy, was the first to arrive. "Kelly, what's going on?" Before she could tell him, paramedics and police filled the room. Rich and several others had their guns drawn and pointed at Deidre. "Call the dogs off, Kelly, we've got her. I need you to tell me what happened."

She gave Rebel the command, "Stand Down." He backed off of Deidre and Lady, following Rebel's lead, let go of her pant leg. Kelly turned to a paramedic who was taking Mike's vital signs, "Is he going to be all right?"

"Yes, ma'am. He's got a huge knot on his head where it looks like he was hit with some kind of a blunt instrument. He's going to have a nasty headache tomorrow, but other than that, I think he's going to be fine."

Rebel went over to Mike, licking his face and making whimpering sounds. He knew Mike was hurt, he just didn't know how badly. Lady stood next to Kelly, as if to protect her in case she needed it.

When the paramedics started to wheel Mike out of the room after they'd put him on a gurney, Kelly asked "Where are you taking him?"

"The hospital in Sunset Bay. We need to take x-rays and make sure he doesn't have a concussion."

"All right. Just a moment." She took her phone out of her purse and called Doc. "It's Kelly. Mike's been hurt. The paramedics are taking him to the hospital in Sunset Bay for x-rays. Would you go there and treat him? I'll meet you as soon as I can get there. Thanks." She turned to the paramedic who seemed to be in charge and told him Dr. Burkhart was on his way to the hospital and not to do anything until he arrived and that she'd be there as soon as she could.

Deidre was sitting on the floor with her back against the wall, muttering to herself. Her hands were behind her back, secured by handcuffs. Rich motioned Kelly over. "What happened? She's muttering something about feet and shoes and Scott and Mike. It's as if she's snapped."

They both were quiet as they stood and looked down at Diedre. She seemed to have retreated into a world of her own and was no longer part of the world around her. They overheard her saying, "I told you I was going to kill you, Mike. You're just like Scott. He wouldn't have me either and neither would those other men, but I got them, all of them. Just like Momma always told me that my feet were pretty, I told them the same thing before I killed them. Then I took pictures of their feet. That way, they're still alive because I have pictures of their feet."

Kelly and Rich exchanged glances of disbelief. "Kelly, what happened before we got here?" She told him everything from the moment she'd pulled in the lot at city hall up to now. He continued,

"I know you want to get to the hospital and be with Mike, but I need to write up a report for you to sign and get a statement from him. I don't want to keep you now. How about if I come over later tonight?"

"Let me call you, Rich. I have no idea how long Doc will want to keep Mike under observation. Unless he has a concussion, I'd think he could come home tonight, but I don't know if she did something else to him. I guess we won't know any more about what happened before I got here until we hear from Mike."

"Kelly, I'm taking Deidre to the station, but I want Dave to drive you to the hospital in your minivan and then you'll have it there to take Mike home when Doc releases him. One of the other deputies will follow and bring Dave back. They'll get Mike's car to your house. I've got a duplicate key in the office for it. You've been through a lot in the last hour, so take a deep breath, try to relax and thank your lucky stars that you showed up when you did. Clearly, you and the dogs saved Mike's life. When you leave here, Lady and Rebel can go with you. Don't think anyone at the hospital will tell you no dogs allowed considering you'll be visiting the county sheriff and Rebel's his dog."

"Well, I guess he is Mike's dog now, but I'm pretty proud of Lady. She sure wanted to help and it seemed like she knew what to do. Neither one of those dogs hesitated for a second. I'm just glad Deidre's front door was unlocked. If it hadn't been, we may have been going to the morgue rather than the hospital."

"Glad it's the hospital."

"Me too!" Rebel and Lady both let out a bark as if they perfectly understood the conversation."

CHAPTER TWENTY-SIX

Three hours later Kelly and Rich, who Kelly had called from the hospital when they were getting ready to leave Sunset Bay, helped a still very drowsy Mike into the house and into his favorite chair by the window. With the time spent taking x-rays and talking to Doc, along with everything else that had happened, Mike had missed the sunset by more than an hour. Fortunately the x-rays had shown that there was no skull fracture and Mike didn't even have a concussion.

Rebel sensed something had happened to Mike and sat down next to him, whimpering. Mike reached down, petted him, and began to talk.

"Kelly, what happened? I remember getting out of my car to go into Deidre's apartment building and rolling the window down so Rebel could get some air. I didn't expect to be gone very long. When I was walking up the steps to the front door, I felt something hard jabbed in my side and heard Deidre tell me to walk to the elevator, that she'd been waiting for me. She said she had a gun in my side and if she shot it, no one would hear it because she had a silencer on it. I remember yelling 'On Guard' to Rebel. Deidre opened the door of her apartment and I saw my photographs on the wall and none of Scott.

"She said something like, 'I'm giving you one more chance to be with me rather than Kelly.' I remember shaking my head and saying no. She started talking, almost like someone who had lost her mind. She said she'd asked Scott to be with her when he was doing the walking meditation and when he said no, she'd pulled her gun out of the waistband of her yoga pants and shot him. She said she'd asked him before and if he wouldn't be with her, she'd make certain he'd never be with anyone. She said she'd done the same thing to the guy in Arizona when he wouldn't leave his wife for her and it was time for her to do the same to me, but first she needed to take pictures of my feet. That's the last thing I remember. She must have hit me on the head with the pistol. The next thing I remember is waking up in the hospital with you and Doc next to my bed. Want to tell me what happened in the interim?"

"I think you're very lucky the only lasting thing from your meeting with Deidre is going to be a big lump on your head for a while. Doc says it looks like a giant goose egg. He gave me some pain pills for you."

"How did you get there? And what about Deidre?"

Rich interrupted, "Mike, Kelly, I'm recording this. Just want to make sure it's okay with you. I'd appreciate it if I can get it on record that you both gave me permission to record this conversation. Thanks."

Kelly told Mike about noticing his patrol car on the street and seeing Rebel in it and it looked like he was barking, which was unusual. She said she heard Rebel as soon as the door of her minivan was opened. Kelly told him how she'd unlocked his patrol car and let Rebel out, then she described what had happened from the time they'd entered the apartment building until she went to the hospital to meet Doc.

"Mike, you're lucky to be alive. If I hadn't decided to renew my driver's license and seen your car with Rebel in it and acting strange, I don't know what would have happened. Deidre snapped or had a mental breakdown or whatever you want to call it. When I left for the hospital, she was muttering about killing Scott and a bunch of other men, even that guy in Arizona you told me about. I have no idea how many men she's killed. Evidently she stalked them and when they either became afraid of her or turned her down, she killed them. She was talking about taking pictures of their feet."

"Good grief. I wondered where my shoes and socks were. Do you know what happened to them?"

"Yes. She was in the process of removing them from your feet when we got there. There was no point in putting them on when you were in the hospital, so I brought them home. Here they are."

"I don't think I want them now. Whenever I put them on, I'd only think of Deidre." He turned to Rich, "What did you do with her?"

"I took her to the station and booked her. Then I put her in isolation because she seemed to have suffered a complete mental breakdown. She was about as loony as anyone I've ever seen. I'm no expert on mental illness, but I'd say she's had a major break with reality. She keeps muttering about the men she's killed and feet and all kinds of other weird stuff. It's Friday night so she won't be arraigned until Monday."

"What will happen to her then?" Kelly asked.

"She's entitled to a public defender," Rich said, "and usually in cases like this, she'll plead not guilty and given the circumstances of the case, the judge will probably send her to the state mental hospital for a psychiatric evaluation. Between what she's admitted to and her obvious mental state, I don't think she'll be back on the streets for a long time. The whole thing is downright weird."

"Mike," Kelly said, "I thought we had a deal. I promised to keep my gun on me at all times and you promised to have Rebel with you at all times. Why wasn't he with you?"

At his name being mentioned, Rebel's ears perked up. It seemed as if he, too, was waiting for Mike to answer and was wondering the same thing.

"I decided to let him stay in my patrol car. I figured I wouldn't be gone long. I was simply going to meet with Deidre and take a routine statement from her. I didn't think I'd need Rebel with me. It never occurred to me that I could be in danger. I mean, who would expect a beautiful young woman to be a killer?"

"Well, it's rather obvious you didn't. I'm just glad your bad experience had such a happy outcome."

"Believe me, you're not the only one."

They were interrupted by Kelly's cell phone ringing. She pulled it out of her purse and answered it. "Hi, Doc. Thanks again for taking care of Mike." She listened for a minute. "Sure, you can talk to him. He's wide awake." She handed the phone to Mike.

"Thanks, Doc. I felt a lot better when I came to and saw you next to my hospital bed. I knew I was in good hands, but you don't need to spend your weekend time calling to see how I'm doing. Honest, I'm fine." A moment later he said, "You didn't call to see how I'm doing? You called to see if I would be the best man in your wedding? What are you talking about?"

Kelly started crying when she overheard Mike's conversation with Doc. What with the events of the day and now the good news that Doc and Liz were going to get married, she gave in to the tears that had been hovering at the edges of her eyes for some time. Mike pushed the end call button on his phone and said, "Did you know he was going to ask Liz to marry him tonight?"

"Yes, he was in the coffee shop earlier today and he showed me the diamond ring he bought for her. What an ending to this week! You're almost killed and Doc's going to get married. Don't think I could have scripted this one."

"Kelly, the longer I'm around you the less surprised I am at how things always seem to turn out all right when you're involved."

"Well, Sheriff Mike, since we're in a two week countdown until our wedding, you have one thing to do between now and then, and that's rest and get rid of what looks like a large appendage growing out of the back your head. Some wedding pictures those will be if that thing's not gone in two weeks."

"Time for me to leave," Rich said. "Other than that huge thing on your head, Mike, I think you're going to be okay. Kelly, Mike, I'll have the conversation I recorded transcribed and then you both can sign it."

"No problem," Mike said.

"By the way, the other deputies and I will be taking turns working overtime for the next few days so you can get some rest. We all want to see you looking good at the wedding." Rich turned to Kelly. "Mike, time for you to get in bed. I think that's a real good place for you to be until you get back to normal. Okay with you, Kelly, if I help cart him off to bed?"

"Yes. That's an excellent idea. He can stay there all weekend and I'll wait on him like I'm his own personal slave."

"I'd like that," Mike said. "Probably be the last time that'll happen."

"You got that right, Sheriff Mike, so don't get used to it. This is a one-time only kind of thing. Now, down the hall with you. I'll bring you something to eat a little later."

Rebel followed Rich and Mike down the hall. When they were gone, Lady looked up at Kelly as if to say, "Remember me? I'm the one who also helped save Mike's life. I think a special treat is in order. What do you think?"

"Lady, good job. I think I have a little piece of roast beef in the refrigerator that just might have your name on it. Rather imagine you'd enjoy it. You deserve it. Thanks, girl." Lady wagged her tail and followed Kelly to the refrigerator. If dogs could grin, she clearly had an ear-to-ear grin on her face.

EPILOGUE

GUIDO

Phew, he thought as he cleared airport security, *it's a lot easier when you don't have to worry about sneaking a gun through. Glad I left it with the Pellino Brothers. Since they're part of the Family, they can probably find a use for it. I mean, I like to pop someone as much as any other hit man who works for the Family, but poppin' some spiritual idol? I dunno, maybe it's that church upbringin' Mom forced on us kids, but killing some Zen Master who wears robes, well, just glad I didn't have to do it.*

I was all set to pop the good Zen Master during the walking meditation when I followed him down the trail he took and hid in the bushes next to the trail, waiting for him to return. All I had to do was just step out of the bushes, hold my .22 right next to his head, and bingo, the job's done. Figured by the time all the dust settled I'd be sittin' on a plane headed back to Chicago. Then all of a sudden along comes that crazy redhead broad running down the trail in the direction of the Zen Master. Good thing I stayed hidden, because the next thing I know, that dumb sheriff is hotfootin' it down the trail and I overhear some students say the Zen Master has been shot and killed. Always a little easier when someone else takes care of the Family's business. Odds are my next hit won't be some spiritual guru and it will just be business as usual.

Looking forward to goin' home. Lotta people don't like Chicago in January, but it's better than the damp cold out here in the Pacific Northwest. Anyway, the kids and wife'll be happy to see me. Yeah, it's good to be going home and not havin' to look over my shoulder.

DANTE AND LUCA

They were glad Guido had gone back to Chicago right after the murder of Scott Monroe. He was a cold-blooded killer working for the Family and they were frightened just being around him. However, they had to agree that his idea to become one of the Zen Master's students so he could get close to Scott and be ready on a moment's notice to complete the assignment Mr. Rossi had given him, was pure genius.

The Pellino brothers were certain that the high-end pinot noir wine they were getting ready to introduce would make the Pellino Brothers Vineyard synonymous with the best pinot noir wine in Oregon. They expected some disarray at the White Cloud Retreat Center and vineyard because of the murder of Scott Monroe, its founder and head wine-maker. They hoped his death would help the sale of their wines. With Scott gone and his fine wines presumably on hiatus, they were sure they'd be able to convince The Crush's owner, Jesse, to carry their wines and help make them a household word in the local area and all of Oregon. They knew they had to succeed in order to maintain Mr. Rossi's faith in them or otherwise they might be on the receiving end of a visit from Guido, which was not a pleasant thought.

DOC

A reconciliation with his sons, a restored medical license, and now engaged to the town psychologist – life was definitely looking up for Doc Burkhart. Planning a wedding, more visits from his sons, and enlarging his medical practice was keeping him very busy. His fiancée, Liz, was trying to talk him into taking up boating, telling him how much his sons would enjoy it when they came to visit, but he didn't think that was going to happen given his life-long fear of the ocean. The gift he'd received from Kelly, the yellow Labrador named Lucky, was growing up to be a very faithful friend to his master.

LUKE

Luke called Kelly a few days after Deidre had been arrested to tell her he'd decided to stay on at the White Cloud Retreat Center and take over Scott's position as Zen Master. He told her that although he'd written some phony checks to a fake business he'd opened up so he could siphon money out of the Center's bank account without Scott finding out, a few days after Scott died he'd been meditating and had a moment of enlightenment that was life-changing.

He returned all of the money he'd taken from the Center and gave up any ideas he'd had about escaping to Mexico. He said he'd decided to continue on with Scott's dream of making White Cloud Retreat Center a haven for all who sought spirituality, as well as a good glass of wine.

Luke told her he'd already asked Jesse at The Crush to give him a crash course in making wine and that Jesse had agreed to help him. He told Kelly he was hoping she'd be coming to the Center to take some more classes and she'd replied that her wedding gift to herself was just that.

JIM

He continued to work for the electric company, troubleshooting wherever he was needed. Fortunately, he'd been able to take care of the electrical service problems the Center was having and never had to return to it. With the Center's problems fixed, he left his .22 pistol at home because the forest area near the Center was the only place he'd ever seen any bears.

The pastor of Jim and Ellie Duncan's church made Jim a lay pastor because of his commitment to the church. He ministered to people who were unable to come to church and on Sundays, was the pastor's right hand man. Ellie was sure his work with the church would assure them both places in heaven and she reminded the Tuesday morning Bible study group of that every week.

DEIDRE

Deidre is now a permanent resident at the large red brick Oregon State Mental Hospital in Salem, Oregon, locked in the high security section reserved for the criminally insane. She spends her days in a world of her own, unreachable through therapy or medication. She was diagnosed as psychotic by psychiatrists at the institution and never stood trial for Scott's or anyone else's murder. Her mutterings indicate she killed many other men over the years, but none of the bodies have ever been recovered, and the photographs of their feet taken from her apartment have been untraceable.

Her pistol with the silencer on it was recovered from her apartment. Ballistic tests confirmed it was the gun used to kill Zen Master Scott.

BLAINE

He returned to the Center a few days after he'd mysteriously left. Blaine told Luke he'd crashed and burned when he ran out of his medication and decided to leave the Center. After he left he'd gotten in touch with the doctor at the Oregon State Mental Hospital where he'd previously been a patient and the doctor had given him several new prescriptions. The new medications worked and he now felt stable, recovered, and ready to go back to work. He asked Luke if he could have a second chance at the Center and told him he'd still very much like to become a Zen priest, but had given up thoughts of becoming a Zen Master. Luke agreed to take him back, but only if he promised to take his medications daily. Blaine promised he would and since he had more experience in the vineyards than any of the other residential trainees, he gladly agreed to be in charge of it.

SHERIFF MIKE

The bump on his head soon went away and he was back at work in a few days, making sure the people of Beaver County and Cedar Bay were safe. There was a hiatus in crime and Mike used the extra time to help Kelly get ready for their upcoming wedding and spend time with her children, Julia and Cash. Rebel had become his constant shadow and it was widely known around town that Rebel could always be seen in the shotgun seat of Sheriff Mike's patrol car, preferably with the window open and his head sticking out, enjoying the sights and smells of the Cedar Bay area.

KELLY

Kelly was glad that for now, there were no serious crimes to investigate and solve in the sleepy little town of Cedar Bay and she could spend her time getting ready for her upcoming wedding. Two of Roxie's friends volunteered to come to Kelly's Koffee Shop the week before the wedding and work so Kelly could take the week off and spend it with her children and taking care of last-minute preparations. It was Roxie's wedding gift to Kelly and it may have been the most thoughtful and appreciated wedding gift she received!

REBEL AND LADY

Rebel continued to show Lady how to be a guard dog by always checking to make sure their masters were safe from danger. When they were together they were inseparable, whether they were eating, sleeping, or playing, but as soon as they got a call from their master, that took precedence over everything else. Sometimes life is just so good you have to smile, and anyone who saw the dogs, swore they were always wearing a friendly smile!

RECIPES

RICOTTA CAKE

Ingredients

1 box yellow or lemon cake mix
1 ¼ cups water
1/3 cup oil
2 lbs. ricotta cheese
1 cup sugar
5 eggs
¼ cup powdered sugar

Directions

Preheat oven to 350 degrees. Prepare cake batter according to package directions mixing together oil, cake mix, water and 3 eggs. Pour into 9 x 13 Pyrex baking dish which has been lightly oiled and floured.

Mix ricotta cheese, sugar and 2 eggs together and pour mixture on top of prepared cake mix, smoothing it out so it's level. Bake one hour. Remove from oven and let cool for 45 minutes. When cool sprinkle with powdered sugar and cut into serving size squares. Enjoy!

SAVORY MINI HAM AND EGG MUFFINS

Ingredients

1/4 baguette loaf or other bread (should be fairly dry) cut/torn
into small pieces
4 oz. of a block of cream cheese, cut crosswise into 12 slices
1 tbsp. olive oil
¼ lb. thinly sliced ham, chopped (about 1 cup) (A left-over
cooked meat may be substituted for the ham, chopped medium
fine) 2 green onions, thinly sliced
1 ½ cups half-and-half
6 eggs
1 tsp. thyme
Salt and pepper to taste

Directions

Preheat oven to 350 degrees.

Using a 12 cup muffin pan, fill each cup half full with bread
pieces. Top each cup with a cream cheese slice. In a small saucepan,
heat olive oil over medium heat and add ham. Cook for 5 minutes.

Stir in half-and-half and bring to a simmer. Remove from heat and
set aside.In a medium bowl, whisk eggs, thyme, and green onions
together, then whisk in the warm half-and-half mixture. Add salt and
pepper.

Pour the egg mixture on top of the bread/cheese in each muffin
cup and bake 15 minutes until puffed up and golden brown around
edges. Remove from oven and let cool for 15 minutes. Run thin knife
around edge of each cup. Remove from muffin pan and serve. Enjoy!

DOC'S OVEN BEEF BURGUNDY   (Serves Six)

Ingredients

3 lbs. beef stew meat, cubed. I use boneless chuck roast.
2 large onions, sliced
1 garlic clove, minced
3 tbsp. soy sauce
¼ tsp. thyme
1 ½ cups sliced mushrooms
3 tbsp. flour
¼ tsp. Tabasco sauce
¼ tsp. marjoram
1 cup red wine

Directions

Preheat oven to 325 degrees.

Blend soy sauce and flour together in large ovenproof deep baking dish. Add cubed meat, toss, coating all pieces. Add onions, seasonings and wine to meat mixture. Stir and bake, covered, for one hour.

Remove from oven and stir. Return to oven and bake, covered, for another hour.

Remove from oven and stir in mushrooms. Return to oven and bake, covered, for the last hour. Total cooking time is three hours.

Serve over Doc's Buttered Noodles. Enjoy!

DOC'S NO-FAIL BUTTERED NOODLES

Ingredients

2 chicken bouillon cubes (I use Wyler's)
1 ½ cups water

1 stick unsalted butter 8 oz. egg noodles

Directions

In a large saucepan, bring water, bouillon cubes, and ½ stick of butter to a boil over medium to high heat. Add egg noodles and cook to desired texture, approx. 6-8 minutes. Divide remaining ½ stick of butter into 3-5 pieces and stir into hot noodles until the butter is completely melted.

Remove from pan and serve with Doc's Oven Beef Burgundy. Enjoy!

CHARLIE'S SAUSAGE GRAVY WITH BISCUITS

Ingredients

16 oz. package of Jimmy Dean sausage (sage flavor)2 tbsp. ground sage
2 tbsp. Wondra flour
1 pint heavy whipping cream
1 roll of refrigerated biscuits (large flaky type)

Directions

Bake the biscuits according to the directions on the package.

While the biscuits are in the oven, tear the sausage into bite size pieces and place in a large frying pan. The pieces should nearly cover the bottom of the pan. Shake the ground sage evenly over the uncooked pieces and fry the sausage over medium high heat, turning the pieces so each pieceis evenly browned - about 5 minutes.

Push the cooked sausage to one side of the pan and tilt pan to the opposite side, allowing the sausage grease to collect on the empty side of the pan. Shake the Wondra flour into the grease and stir with fork for 1 minute. Combine the sausage and flour mixture and slowly add the cream, approximately 1/3 at a time, until all the cream has been added. Reduce the heat to medium and stir until the mixture becomes a thick gravy (about 3-5 minutes). Add more flour as needed to make it thicker.

Remove biscuits from oven and break in half. Spoon the sausage gravy over each biscuit half. Enjoy!

ABOUT THE AUTHOR

Dianne lives in Huntington Beach, California with her husband Tom, a former California State Senator, and her new boxer puppy, Kelly. Her passions are cooking and dogs and whenever she has a little free time, you can find her in the kitchen or in the yard throwing a ball. She is a frequent contributor to the Huffington Post.

Her other award winning books include:

Kelly's Koffee Shop
Murder at Jade Cove

Blue Coyote Motel
Coyote in Provence
Cornered Coyote

Tea Party Teddy
Tea Party Teddy's Legacy

Website: www.dianneharman.com
Blog: www.dianneharman.com/blog
Email: dianne@dianneharman.com

Made in the USA
Lexington, KY
21 May 2015